The Loner

D0982170

The Loner

Ester Wier

AN
APPLE
PAPERBACK

SCHOLASTIC INC.
New York Toronto London Auckland Sydney

No part of this publication may be reproduced in whole or in part, or stored in a retrieval system, or transmitted in any form or by any means, electronic, mechanical, photocopying, recording, or otherwise, without written permission of the publisher. For information regarding permission write to Scholastic Inc., 730 Broadway, New York, NY 10003.

ISBN 0-590-44352-6

Copyright © 1963, 1991 by Ester Wier. All rights reserved. Published by Scholastic Inc., 730 Broadway, New York, NY 10003, by arrangement with the Author. APPLE PAPERBACKS is a registered trademark of Scholastic Inc.

24 23 22 21 20 19 18 17 16 15 14   8 9/9 0/0

Printed in the U.S.A.   40

The
Loner

1

The boy had been traveling with the old man for two months, time enough to have grown used to the wavering and unsteady gait of the truck. It still made him uneasy, crawling along the highways like a wounded animal, from one crop-picking station to the next. They had gone from Alabama to South Carolina to Louisiana. Now they were headed for Texas and the bean fields, and after that they would go wherever there was work, wherever there were crops to be picked and people needed to pick them.

Traveling with the old man wasn't too bad. He'd had worse to put up with, worse than the old man's foggy ways, worse than the old man's living in a world of his own. The old man spent most of his time mumbling words and names that meant nothing to anyone but himself and he seldom bothered to listen to what anyone else said.

Long ago the boy had made up his mind that

the only way to get along in the world was to look out for himself. He decided this when he found out that no one else was going to do it for him. Sometimes he thought he remembered his mother taking care of him; other times he was certain he had made her up just to have someone who belonged to him. He had no way of knowing what had happened to her or his father. Perhaps they had died. All he was really sure of was that he had worked in the fields for almost as long as he could remember, that many different families had let him travel with them, taking his earnings in return for a place to sleep, something to eat, a way to get from crop field to crop field. Living with them had taught him that when he wanted something bad enough, he could put up with almost anything to get it.

And so right now he wanted the transportation the old man's truck offered. He longed to get to California and if he stayed with the old man he would get there, eventually. So even things like the old man's pocketing his earnings, instead of buying food with it as they'd agreed, didn't worry him except when they ran out of food entirely. He didn't blame the old man. He was just looking out for himself.

The boy's life now was about the same as it had been with the last people he had traveled with, the ones who had left him behind in Florida when he was getting over the fever. They'd had to take

2

care of themselves, too. Sick as he was, he remembered them standing over him as he lay on
the floor of the tar-paper shack on an old blanket.
They were arguing.

"We've got to take him," the woman had said.
"We can't leave him here alone."

The man wouldn't listen. "My job is findin' work
for you and me, not takin' care of some stray who
don't belong to us."

The woman pleaded. "Then let's get someone
from town out here and see that they put him in
a home or somewhere."

The man raised his voice angrily. "I'm not gettin' tangled up with any of them do-gooders.
We've got to be movin' north where there's crops
to be picked. If them folks come out here, they'll
start askin' questions and we'll never get away.
Don't know why I ever let him ride with us in the
first place."

The woman was spunky. She didn't give up
easy. "We could take him along. He won't eat
much while he's sick like this and, when he gets
well, there'd be his pickin' money too."

But her husband put his foot down. "I ain't sad-
dlin' myself with a runt of a boy who won't be
worth any keep at all for weeks to come, and you
ain't gonna have time to nurse him. You'll be out
pickin' crops and that's the last I'm gonna say
about it."

Even while he hoped and prayed they'd take

3

him with them, the boy felt the man was right. Being left alone and sick in a deserted pickers' camp wasn't anything to look forward to, but he didn't blame them. They had to look out for themselves.

He'd made out all right. They had stayed with him until his fever broke and then left a blanket over him and a can of water within his reach. The woman had tucked a loaf of bread under the blanket, and a pile of pennies so he could buy food. He was sure the man hadn't known about the money. She'd probably been saving it for something she wanted. He was grateful, but her kindness surprised him.

Once the fever went down, he got well fast. He was thin and wiry and strong. The potatoes that had spilled out of someone's sack and were lying by the drainage ditch between the shacks had kept him going, and he had bought some meat with the money and made himself a stew. It lasted several days. Finally, when he was strong enough, he hitched his way to Alabama. There were always workers who would give a boy a lift from one harvest to another without asking questions.

The only thing the old man who picked him up in Alabama asked him was his age.

The boy shrugged his thin shoulders. "I don't know. Nobody ever told me."

"Reason I asked," the old man explained, "is

4

that some places they won't let you pick unless you're fourteen." He looked the boy over. "You're a mite little for fourteen but we can tell them you were the runt of the litter." The old man thought that was a fine joke and he chuckled over it for a long time.

Now they were headed for Texas in a caravan of trucks. The boy knew he was lucky to be riding on a seat of boards beside the old man. On the back of the other trucks, the children were loaded like cattle, jammed in with old foot lockers, oil-stoves, rusty bedsprings, washtubs, and carton boxes.

Some of the places they stopped for food wouldn't serve them. "Move on," they were told, and then it might be hours before they found a place willing to sell them food to eat in the truck.

Local police often followed them, turning back only when the broken-down, shabby caravan was safely beyond the town limits.

Around noon one day two of the trucks stopped for gas, along with other necessities, at a station on the outskirts of a town. While the old man talked to the attendant, the boy slipped carefully around the building to get a drink of water from the fountain outside the rest rooms. He'd just reached it when a station worker leaped to bar his way.

"Trash!" he shouted. "Get your filthy self back

5

to that truck where it belongs. We don't want you disease carriers around here." The boy clenched his fists, anger flashing in his eyes.

"I only want a drink of water," he said.

The man was big and ugly and he came forward with his hand raised. Someone pulled the boy backward and he swung around to find a girl tugging at his shirt.

"Come on," she said, and led him away. "You'll only make it so's we can't even buy gas if you cause trouble. Can't you see he's just spoilin' for a fight? Some folks don't want anything to do with us crop-pickers and they'll do everything against us except refuse to take our money. When they won't take our money any longer, then it'll be real bad."

She was bigger than he was, with her long yellow hair pulled back and tied with a string behind her head. She led him to her father's truck and pulled a gray-filmed bottle from under the old quilts piled on the back. The water was warm and brackish but he drank it gratefully.

"There's a spring up a ways on the road so you can get more then," she told him. "We come this way most nearly every year and I always wait to get to that spring. It's the prettiest place I ever saw and the water is cold and sweet. It comes right out of the ground and then runs over some stones and off into the woods. Now, just follow us

6

and stop when we do. My pa says we'll fill all our bottles there."

"What's your name?" he asked.

She smiled at him. "Raidy," she said. "Short for Radelia. My ma thought it up and I guess no one in the world has a name like it."

When they started off again, he told the old man about the spring. "My friend says it's good and cold." The word slipped out before he knew it and he realized it was the first time in his life he had thought of anyone as his friend.

The old man grunted, his small eyes inflamed with the dust and the heat and fixed as usual on some far-off place. They followed behind the truck Raidy was on and she sat watching him, her body swaying to the truck's rhythm, her bare feet swinging over the edge of the rear platform. Her yellow hair gleamed in the sun. The old man's truck zigzagged along the road, straying perilously across the center line at times.

When the truck Raidy was on moved off the highway toward a clump of trees, the boy called out for the old man to turn, but they kept to the road. The old man didn't even hear him. He went on mumbling to himself and kept his foot on the gas pedal.

They hadn't gone a hundred yards when the boy heard a siren behind them and turned to see a state trooper's car.

7

"It's cops!" he cried.

The siren continued to sound, loud and insistent, and at last it got through the clouds in the old man's mind. "Blast!" he said, putting his foot on the brake. The truck wheezed to a faltering stop and the boy moved close to the door. While the old man leaned out to watch the trooper approach, he opened the door and leaped to the highway, dropping into a ditch beside it.

He lay there listening. "What kind of driving do you call that?" the trooper asked. "I've been watching and your truck's been all over the road. Well, I can get rid of old bums like you in one of two ways, either keep you moving until you're out of my territory or take you to jail. I'd be doing everyone on the road a favor if I locked you up."

The old man protested loudly. "I ain't hit nobody yet!" he shouted. "Why don't you pick on someone your own age? Whatcha doin'? Tryin' to fill your quota of arrests for the month? You make me sick."

The boy knew the trooper wouldn't take talk like that.

"All right, it's back to the station for you. Maybe you'll cool off there."

No one missed him. The old man was too busy yelling, and the trooper hadn't even seen him, sitting there too small to be noticed from the rear. The boy lay without moving until they were gone, then rose cautiously, to see the empty truck pushed from the highway, abandoned.

Heading back toward the clump of trees off the road, he walked until he found the spring. Raidy was there and she ran to him, laughing with delight. "I thought they might take you, too," she said. "I was watchin' and I was afraid you'd never get your drink of spring water." She dipped it out for him in a tin can and he drank his fill of the cold sweet water, gasping between swallows. The trees hung low about the spring, forming a secret place, cool and mysterious, smelling of foliage and earthy dampness.

"Wasn't no reason for me to get taken, too," he told her. He hadn't even thought of staying with the old man or trying to help him. When people got mixed up with the police, they had to answer questions, and he wasn't taking any chances of being sent to a children's home somewhere when they found out he didn't have any folks or a home. He had to think of himself and getting to California. The old man could take care of himself.

When it was time to move on, it was Raidy who begged him to go with them. She told her father, "He's got nowheres else to go and there might as well be ten as nine of us. He's little and he won't take up much space. And he needs someone to look out for him."

The boy didn't like that. "I don't need anyone

to look out for me," he told Raidy's father. "I can get along just fine alone."

The man looked at him and smiled. "Now, now," he said, "there's no need for you to be that kind of proud. Everybody needs someone, like them dogs and cats and birds Raidy's always pickin' up. They need her to watch out for them. You willin' to give me your pickin' money if you stay with us?"

He thought it over, then nodded. It was fair enough. He needed a way to travel and they could use the money he earned.

"What about the old man? He your father?"

"No kin," the boy said.

"Will he be catchin' up with us in time, you reckon?"

"Guess so. Probably show up when they let him out of jail."

He stayed with Raidy and her family, picking beans in Texas. Because he'd never picked beans before, the girl stayed right beside him and helped him at first. "I hate them," he told her. "There's so many on the vine." It took forever, it seemed, to pull off enough to fill a hamper. But because he was used to hard work, he kept at it and pretty soon he did it well, picking up to sixteen hampers a day.

The old man hadn't shown up when the bean picking was over so he moved north with Raidy's family to pick beets in Utah, and then potatoes in Idaho. Traveling with them was all right. He gave Raidy's father his picking money and in turn they let him share the floor of an old Quonset hut in Texas, an abandoned railroad boxcar in Utah, and a shack in a growers' camp in Idaho. And they fed him along with the family, thin, watery stews that Raidy's mother and grandmother cooked after their days in the field.

He preferred picking the potatoes because he'd picked them in North Carolina and knew how. Side by side, he and Raidy made a race of it. They grabbed the wooden baskets and burlap sacks and ran to the rows behind the digging machine. Stooping, crawling, sweating, they worked in silence, emptying the heavy baskets into the sacks and running back to fill another and another. It took two baskets to fill a bag, and they got seven cents for every bag filled. When the digging machine broke down, they dropped to the earth, panting for breath, resting until it was repaired or replaced. And always Raidy was laughing and teasing and driving him on to outpick her.

"Pa says it's a lucky day I found you," she said. "You're a good worker because you move fast and you hardly ever complain."

When they weren't working, they talked. Raidy told him about the time she had gone to school. "It was in Oregon and folks there really wanted to help us crop-pickers. They didn't act like the people who yell at you and drive you out of town. Even our teacher liked us. She let us play on the swings in the yard.

"Can you write?" she asked him suddenly.

He shook his head.

"Then I'll teach you." Raidy drew letters for him in the dirt and began to teach him their names. The boy could tell she loved the letters, for she drew them carefully, taking a long time to make them exactly right.

When she found out he didn't have a name, she was horrified. "Even dogs have names," she said.

"Nobody ever called me anything that I can remember, 'cept 'Boy' or 'Hey, You.' "

Raidy explained to him how important a name was. It gave you a feeling of being someone, not just a stray. "If you had a name it would make you feel good."

"Who's going to give me a name?" he scoffed. "I don't have a mother to make up a special one for me."

With quick understanding warmth, she caught his hand. "I'll find you a name," she promised. "I'll have to do some real hard thinkin' about it but I'll find you just the right name."

After that, she would often look at him and say a name, trying it on him for size, then shake her head. "It'll come. The right one will come." She worked hard at putting letters together in the dirt but the results didn't please her. "It'll come," she said, smiling at him, "and when it does, it'll be something special. It's the most important thing I've ever done in my life and I want to do it right."

Then, one morning as they rode the ancient bus that carried them from their camp to the fields, her eyes shone with excitement.

"I got your name," she whispered, but when he asked her what it was, she shook her head. "I'm thinkin' about it. I'll try it out for a while and if I still like it after that, I'll tell you what it is."

They had just started a new row behind the digging machine. As usual Raidy was first and he was close behind her. She turned to him suddenly. "If I tell you now what it is, will you — " She screamed. Leaping forward, he saw that her yellow hair was caught in the whirring moving parts of the machine. Powerless to help, he stood and watched in cold horror while the machine ripped and tore.

After they'd taken her away and the crowd had gone back to work, he went on picking the potatoes mechanically, numb with grief and anger. "Why didn't she take care of herself instead of worrying about my old name?" he thought. "It wouldn't have happened if she had been taking care of herself, not me." But if she had been the kind to think only about herself, she wouldn't have been Raidy, and he wouldn't have liked being with her so much.

He worked the rest of the day without saying a word to anyone. Then he took his day's wages and started walking. He didn't want to look at Raidy's mother and father and grandmother and aunt and brothers and sisters ever again. He wanted to get to California as fast as he could.

2

The boy stood in the middle of the road, gazing up at the wedge of wild geese high in the sky above him. Their noisy honking broke the immense quiet that lay like a blanket, spread from the mountains beyond to the endless plains far below. He turned slowly, watching the birds disappear to the south, thinking how Raidy would have liked seeing them. She would have made up something about them, like saying they were an Indian arrowhead flung across the sky by some unseen arm behind the mountains.

He shook his head dully, pushing Raidy out of his mind, and looked down at his feet. There was little left of the sneakers now, only the ragged canvas around his ankles, the raveled strings which held them on, and what had not been gouged from the soles on the long walk from the highway many miles behind him now.

A late afternoon wind was rising, biting into his

legs through the threadbare dungarees and into his body under the worn flannel shirt. The crack in his lower lip opened again and his tongue, touching it, tasted blood. He put a chapped hand against his lip and pressed hard. Every inch of his body ached, ached with weariness and hunger and the terrible emptiness of losing Raidy.

Beyond him the road climbed another hill and upon the crest spruce trees bent in the wind and shadows spread like dark water seeping from the mountainside. The ruffled edges of the clouds had turned gold and for a moment it seemed that the whole world had become golden, the dried slopes about him reflecting the coming sunset. He was used to being out of doors at all hours but he had never seen anything like this, and he stood, swaying wearily, caught by its splendor. In the distance, off to his right, a herd of deer, driven from the higher ridges by the first signs of winter, moved slowly across the bronze grass. Except for birds, they were the first signs of life he had seen in days of struggling through this country, and suddenly the enormity of the space around him and the loneliness of its silence became more than he could stand, and he found himself running toward the animals, leaving the road and scrambling over sun-scorched pasture land in a fury of haste.

"Wait!" he called, fighting through bushes and over hillocks. "Wait!" he shouted foolishly with all his strength, his voice carrying through the thin air. The deer poised for a moment and then faded into the landscape. He watched them go, still calling frantically and running toward them. They were alive and at this moment he needed to be near something living, something besides endless stretches of hills and plains.

When he realized they were gone, his breath began to come in long, shaking sobs. The reserve strength he had called on in trying to reach them left him, and he fell headlong on the earth beside a cluster of pale-gold serviceberry bushes. The impact knocked the air out of him and he lay without moving, his tear-streaked face pressed into the rough dry grass.

A Montana mountain rat, busy on an errand of nest-making, paused and sat on her haunches, looking at him, before scurrying on across the fields, and a flock of crows flew above him, seeking their roost for the night.

Finally the boy tried to raise his body, his shaggy brown hair falling over his eyes. He couldn't go any farther. He was through, finished, beaten. How long had it been since he left the potato fields and started off on his own across this unfamiliar country? How many rides had he hitched on the highway? Which way was he headed now? How many meals had he made on berries and the raw potatoes he carried in his

17

pockets? He didn't know. He didn't care. Nothing mattered now.

He lay quietly until the sobs began again, deep and racking. Above him the sky turned from gold to dark blue and the clouds drifted to the south. He burrowed deeper into the earth, rolling his body into a ball against the bushes, the weariness spreading through him like a soothing syrup. He cried himself out and slowly his hands relaxed and his eyes closed. Like a small animal seeking the warmth of the earth, he pressed his face against the grass and slept.

The woman, waiting on the rise of the hill, stood six-foot-two in her boots. They were sturdy leather boots, laced to the knee. Above them she wore wool trousers and a heavy wool-lined jacket. On her head was a man's old felt hat, pulled down to cover her ears and the gray hair cut short all over her head. From a distance it would have been hard to tell she was a woman, for her body was powerful and she stood with the grace of an athlete, relaxed yet disciplined. She lifted a hand and called, "Come!" and the dog, below the hill beside some serviceberry bushes, raised his head and looked at her. The rough coat of the collie was black with white markings on the chest, the neck, the legs, and the feet. He stood thirty inches at the shoulder and his weight was nearly eighty pounds. The bigness of his mistress would have dwarfed most dogs, but not Jupiter. He came from a line of the finest sheep dogs of northern Scotland, and it showed in his deep chest, his remarkable height, his proud balance of body.

He looked at the woman and took a few steps toward her, then flung his head high and growled low in his throat. He retraced his steps to the bushes and looked at her again. Barking for a sheep dog was always the last resort in an emergency and one sure to excite the sheep, so he held his voice deep in his throat, and the sound carried no farther than to the woman on the hill.

"What is it, Jup?" she asked, watching him. "If I walk down there and find it's only a rabbit, I'll skin you alive."

The dog, hearing her voice, started toward her again, then stopped and flung his head high.

"All right, all right," she said, "I'm coming."

He met her halfway and led her back to the bushes where the boy lay. There was no surprise on the woman's face. She had lived too long in this vast and unpredictable land to question what happened here. Although her son's death two years before had shaken the very foundations on which her life was built, she still held to her belief in a wisdom greater than man's. "God moves in a mysterious way His wonders to perform," she marveled now. How else had the boy been led here, a stone's throw from the only human being within miles?

"Well," she said at last, "if it were a sheep and as scrawny as this, I'd say it was hardly worth the finding. How do you suppose he got here, Jup? Where does he belong? Hardly enough clothes or flesh on him to cover his bones. You found a real stray this time."

The wind from the mountains carried the icy threat of snows soon to come. The sunset was over and night blue had spread across the sky. The first stars appeared and the chill turned to raw cold.

"Back to the sheep, Jup," the woman said. "I'll handle this." The collie hesitated for a moment in leave-taking, then sped off toward the bed ground, the white tip of his tail moving through the fast-falling darkness.

The woman bent over the sleeping boy. Traces of tears were on his face, streaks through the dust and dirt. His thin body was curled against the cold, and the straight brown hair hung ragged against his neck. "What a miserable little critter," she said softly. "I wouldn't let a sheep get into such a wretched condition." She studied for a while how to move him, and decided against awakening him. Carefully she placed an arm underneath and slowly raised him so that he lay against her, reminding her of stray lambs she had so often carried back to the fold. He stirred, a long convulsive shudder running through his body, then lay quietly in her arms.

She carried him up the hill and across the hundred yards to the sheep wagon. Jup was waiting for her, his head turned toward her yet his senses alert for any movement among the sheep on the bed ground. They lay, over 900 of them, close together on a slanting rise beside the wagon. Around the bed ground, several feet apart, stood the flags to scare off marauding animals.

The other dog, Juno, sniffed daintily, her nose pointed up at the boy. Her rough white coat moved in the wind and her dark mahogany-colored ears stood three-quarters erect, with the ends tipping forward.

"It's all right," the woman assured her. "Now you two get back to your posts and keep a sharp lookout for coyotes. If they get a sheep tonight, I'll skin you both alive." Jup whined softly and moved toward the sheep, Juno following a parallel course on the opposite side of the flock.

Smoke curled from the stovepipe atop the sheep wagon, drifting south with the wind. The woman mounted the steps to the door, pulling it open carefully so as not to disturb the boy. Once in, she shut it behind her and looked about. The benches on either side of the long, narrow room were hard and bare, so she carried the boy to the end where her bed was built cross-wise into the wagon. She pushed aside the sugan, the heavy square comforter, and laid him on top of the blankets. The room was warm and the boy sighed as he turned over and adjusted himself to the softness.

The woman took off her heavy coat and old felt hat and went to the kerosene stove which stood to the right of the door. Taking a kettle, she poured water into it from a bucket, salted it, and set it on the flame. She seemed to fill the end of the wagon, her head clearing the ceiling by only a few inches. While the water came to a boil, she raised a trapdoor in the long bench on the left and pulled out two wool sacks stuffed with straw, two blankets, and another sugan. She made up a bed quickly on the bench, then returned to the stove and poured cornmeal into the boiling water. When the mush was ready she put it into a bowl and punctured a can of milk. She looked at the sugar and hesitated. She didn't hold with spoiling children with sweets. Even her own son had never been allowed sugar on his mush. Life was a hard business and indulgences led only to softness, and softness to weakness. She didn't believe in weakness. She left the bowl on the stove to keep warm and went back to the bed where the boy lay.

"Come," she said, rousing him. The boy's eyes flew open and he lay staring up at her. Confusion was on his face and a wary look about his eyes. "Here's some food," she said. "You look as if you could stand it." She went back to the stove and picked up the bowl.

The boy sat up and backed into a corner of the bed. He looked around the strange room and then up at the woman again. "Who're you?" he asked.

The woman handed him the bowl and poured milk on the mush. "Eat," she said. "I'll talk while you fill your stomach." She wanted to wash his hands and face before he ate but she knew at the moment his need was more for nourishment than for cleanliness.

"Eat!" she said again. The boy stared at her, then dropped his eyes to the bowl. Picking up the spoon, he began to eat, placing the hot mush in his mouth and swallowing hungrily.

"Take it slow," she said. "There's more if you want it." She sat on the bench and leaned forward. "My dog found you a while ago, and I carried you here and put you to bed. I figured you must be hungry so I fixed you something to eat. And I wanted you to know where you were so that when you woke up in the morning you wouldn't be scared to find yourself here."

The boy listened as he ate. "Who're you?" he asked again.

"You can call me Boss, I guess. It's been years since anyone called me anything else. I've got a flock of sheep outside and this is my wagon, and it's resting on the winter range."

The boy finished the mush and, raising the bowl

to his mouth, licked it clean. The woman refilled it for him.

"Now suppose you tell me what to call you," she said.

The boy looked at her silently for a long time. Distrust and caution played over his face, and Boss had the notion that if he could squirm out of the corner and past her, he would make a dash for the door.

"This ain't a home for children?" he asked.

Boss laughed. "It's a home for me, that's what it is. Now what's your name?"

The boy's eyes narrowed. "Boy," he said. "That's what folks call me, unless they're mad at me."

The woman knew she had been right about his being a stray. He was underfed, uncared for, and didn't even have a name. Right now he looked like a hunted animal, a lonely animal fighting for its life in a world where nobody cared about it. It made her mad all over.

"All right," she said, "I'll call you Boy for now." She knew there was no use asking him questions. Let him settle down and relax first. There would be time enough to find out where he belonged and decide what to do with him later.

She took the bowl back to the stove and filled a pan with water from the kettle. In a corner of the dish cupboard beside the stove she found a towel. She got some soap and carried it all back to him.

"Wet a corner of the towel and wash your face. Then scrub your hands," she said. "And use the soap! I'll find something for you to sleep in."

The boy looked at the water and soap. "Is it Saturday?" he asked. In the crop-pickers' camps no one ever bathed except on Saturday evening.

"No, it isn't Saturday but I want you clean because I'm letting you sleep in my bed tonight. I won't have it messed up with a lot of dirt. Now, get to washing!"

She turned her back on him, lifted the bed she had made to get to the trapdoor of the bench again. When she found the garment she wanted, she came back to him and dropped it on the bed. He had rubbed the wet towel across his face, leaving his neck and ears grimy with dirt. She saw that the palms of his hands were heavily calloused, as though they had blistered and healed again and again, forming heavy pads of thickened skin. "Wipe your hands and get into this shirt."

The boy picked up the nightshirt in surprise. "Take off my clothes? Why?"

"So you'll sleep better," she answered. "Take off everything and put it on. I won't watch you."

She took the pan to the door, opened it, and flung the water out upon the ground. Then she refilled the pan and washed the bowl and spoon he had used. "All right to look now?"

The answer was muffled and she turned to see him struggling into the flannel shirt, his head coming slowly through the open neck.

"It's big," he said. "Is it yours?"

She shook her head. "Belonged to old Bezeleel who used to live here. I found it when I moved in. It's clean."

He pulled the nightshirt around him. "Take off your shoes," she said, "and don't ask me why again." He did as he was told.

"Where you sleeping?" he asked.

She pointed to the wool sacks on the bench. "I'll sleep here tonight, soon as I get my boots off."

"You going to wash and take off your clothes too?"

"I've already washed. I do that as soon as I come in from the range and get the sheep settled. And I don't undress because a good herder never takes his clothes off at night. He sleeps with one ear on the sheep and the other on the dogs, and never knows from one minute to the next when he'll have to get out there and scare off a coyote or two."

"That why Beze — the other sheepherder ain't here no more? 'Cause he took off his clothes and used this nightshirt?"

Boss laughed. He was quick all right. . . . "No, that's not why." She stood up and straightened her bed.

"You'd be a good crop-picker," the boy said, studying her. "You're bigger than most men and you could lift a sack of potatoes easy, or even a full hamper of beans."

The woman knew he had paid her a compliment. So that's where he had come from, she thought. Probably from the potato fields in Idaho. But why is he here and who does he belong to?

She raised the blankets on his bed and told him to crawl under. "It's going to be cold when I turn off the stove, so dig down deep and keep the potatoes warm." She picked up a sack of potatoes and put them under the covers beside him. "When you sleep in this bed, that chore goes with it."

He looked at her as though she were crazy. "Sleep with potatoes? Why?"

"So they won't freeze. Now no more questions. I'll leave the stove on in the morning when I start out. And the window over your bed cracked just enough to give you some air. I'll leave biscuits on the stove and a pot of beans, and the rest of the canned milk. Sleep all you can and I'll see you when I get home at sundown. Don't go outside in those thin clothes."

"Where you going?"

"Out with the sheep. They're ready to leave the bed ground at sunup and they'll graze a few miles from here tomorrow. Now no more questions. Go to sleep."

She turned off the lamp and lay down on the

straw-filled wool sacks, drawing the blankets and sugan over her. She listened for the dogs but heard nothing. Not a sound came from the sheep. The wind was dying down and she thought gratefully that perhaps tonight she would be able to sleep straight through. Jup or Juno would warn her if the coyotes came near, or if the sheep became restless and decided to look for higher ground, or if the lead sheep felt she hadn't had enough grass and set off to find more, with the rest of the flock following her.

She would think what to do with the boy tomorrow while she was out on the range. Right now she was tired and sunup was too few hours away.

3

When the boy awoke in the morning, he was startled by his surroundings. Slowly it came back to him. He lay snug and warm under the blankets, examining the room. Boss had left her bed on the long bench neat, the blankets pulled smooth and the sugan folded lengthwise. The hinged window above his bed was held open a crack by a short stick, and he pulled himself up to look out.

There was no sign of Boss or her sheep, only the hills beyond covered with dried brown grass. He got out of bed and walked the length of the wagon to the window set in the upper half of the door. The view from here was a slope leading down to a stand of trees. A road cut through the middle of them and ended at the foot of the hill on which the wagon stood. There was no sign of life in that direction either, only a light wind bending the trees which stood pale and golden in the

29

thin sunlight. The brush among the trees was a flaming orange, and here and there were wild currant and serviceberry bushes.

He turned to find the beans and a pan of biscuits warm on the stove. There was a note on a piece of paper tacked to the dish cupboard but, since he couldn't read, he only looked at it curiously. Opening a biscuit, he heaped beans into it and ate, standing by the stove, the long flannel nightshirt dropping in folds upon the floor.

The woman called Boss had told him not to go out in his thin clothes. He turned the handle of the door and sniffed the air outside. It was brittle-cold and he withdrew hurriedly. Next, he examined the stove, opened the dish cupboard, then tested the sliding bracket of the lamp, standing on his toes to reach it. Discovering the table hinged to the bed, he lifted it and placed the leg under it upright on the floor. He found that when raised it rested on the two benches, and he lifted and lowered it several times. Seeing the rope ring on the hinged short bench lid, he thrust his finger through it and raised the trapdoor. In the grub box were tins of milk, bags of sugar, beans, coffee, and some dried fruit.

Satisfied, he returned to the bed and slipped under the blankets. It was time to think about where he was and what he should do next. Boss hadn't asked him where he had come from. She wasn't nosy like some of the people who had given him rides along the highway. He had told them all something different, anything that popped into his head, but nothing about Raidy or the digging machine or the pickers' camp. He couldn't talk about that.

He had to be getting on to California, before the winter set in. Somehow he must have got turned in the wrong direction so he would have to go back and find the highway again. He looked around the sheep wagon. It was all right here, nice and warm, and there was plenty of food to eat. Boss was all right, too. She had given him her bed and this nightshirt, and she had even covered him up. No one had ever bothered so much about him before, no one but Raidy. He lay back and closed his eyes, suddenly tired again.

When he awakened, a man was standing in the doorway looking at him. The man was young, with dark weather-beaten skin and very light blue eyes. His clothes were rough and well worn. He held a pipe in one hand and a bag of flour and tins of food under his arm. Closing the door behind him, he came to the short bench and laid the articles on it.

"Where's Boss?" he asked, and the boy immediately knew he was a Texan. He had the same way of saying words, drawling them slow and easy, like the overseers in the bean fields.

He sat up. "Out with the sheep," he said, feeling comfortable with this man right away.

"When I saw smoke from the chimney, I wondered if she was sick." The man removed his greasy hat and extended a hand. "I'm Tex," he said, "camp tender."

His words meant nothing to the boy but they shook hands. "I've got kerosene and wood and more groceries in the truck outside. Some mail here." He removed it from his pocket. "If it's all right with you, I'll make some coffee and warm myself up a bit." Without waiting for a reply, he took off his coat, filled the coffeepot from the bucket, and sprinkled a handful of coffee into the water. Setting it on the stove, he lighted his pipe and sat down on the bench.

"You know what a camp tender is?" he asked.

The boy shook his head.

"My job is to come up here every week to see how Boss is makin' out and to bring provisions. Now, there's snow blowin' up in the northwest so I'm bringin' supplies in early. Tell Boss we're in for some weather, first of the season, and that Bezeleel's dog was rabid. Must have been bit by a coyote before he turned on the old man. And tell her — "

The boy interrupted him. "Who got bit by a coyote?"

"The dog that belonged to the old feller who used to be herder here."

"What's rabid?"

Tex laughed. "You sure got a lot of questions. Say, I thought everyone in Montana knew what rabid meant."

The boy shrugged. "Is that where I am?"

"Sure. Where did you think you were?"

"I didn't know but it didn't seem like what I'd heard about California. Wasn't warm enough. Any crops to pick around here?"

"Whoa, boy. You asked me a question. Rabid means the coyote was sick and he bit the dog and made him sick too, then the dog bit the old man."

"I don't like dogs," the boy said.

Tex looked at him, surprised. "Don't believe I ever knew a boy before who didn't like dogs. I wouldn't let Boss hear you say that. Jup and Juno are the best friends she has. And two of the best sheep dogs in these parts."

"Friends?" the boy said scornfully. "I'd never have a dog for a friend. I been throwing rocks at dogs as long as I can remember. And hitting them, too."

"Why?"

It seemed strange to the boy that Tex didn't know why. "We were both after the same food, that's why." He boasted, "But I usually got it."

Tex stood up and went to the stove. The coffee was boiling and he took a cup from the dish cupboard and filled it with the strong black liquid. When he was sitting down again, he said, "Yes,

33

you're in Montana. But there's no crops to be picked here now. Did you run away?"

The boy considered the question. "No. I just left."

"What about your folks? They'll be worried."

Amazement showed in the boy's eyes. "Worried about me? Nobody's going to be worried about me. I never had any folks."

"Who takes care of you?"

"Takes care of me? I take care of myself, always have."

Tex chuckled. "You sound like a real loner for sure."

"A loner? What's that?"

"Best way I can explain is to tell you how I grew up. I didn't have folk either, nobody to worry about me. I grew up in an orphan's home."

"One of those places?" The boy was horrified.

"Oh, it wasn't so bad. You might say I was a loner, too. One of those who didn't believe anyone cared about them or wanted to help. I figured it was up to me to take care of myself and I didn't need help from anyone."

The boy nodded. This man understood.

"Let me tell you, boy, that's a poor way of livin'. A mighty selfish one, too. Somebody will care if you just give 'em a chance."

The boy thought of Raidy.

"There's always people who need you as much as you need them. Don't you forget that. All you got to do is find 'em. And when you do, you find you're happier carin' about someone else than just about yourself all the time." Tex took another long swallow of hot coffee. "You thinkin' about stayin' around here? This is mighty pretty country. It's sheep country."

The boy thought it over. "I was planning to get on to California but I might stay a little while — if she'll let me."

Tex leaned back and laughed. "You know what I think? I think Boss has got herself a bum lamb."

"What's that?"

Tex raised his eyebrows into an arch. "Guess you don't know nothin' about sheep raisin'. Let's see how I can explain it. At lambin' time in the spring, the ewe — "

"The what?"

"The mother sheep. Well, sometimes her lamb dies. Or sometimes the ewe dies. Now everybody knows ewes are healthier and happier if they've a lamb to raise, and lambs are better off if they've a mother. So the lambers take an orphan lamb — they call 'em bum lambs — and give it to the ewe that lost hers. Understand?"

"Sure," the boy said. "The mother needs a baby and the baby needs a mother so they put them together. The ewe adopts it the way they say people do sometimes for kids in those orphan homes."

Tex shook his head. "That's where you're

wrong. The ewe knows the scent of her own lamb and sometimes she won't take a bum lamb. Sometimes she'll even trample it to death."

"What do they do then?"

"They fool the ewe. They skin her dead lamb and put its wool on the bum. They make slits for the legs and one for the neck and then they slip it over the bum and give him to the ewe. Funniest thing you ever saw. The lamb has two tails and eight legs."

The boy laughed. "Does she take it then?"

"Sure," said Tex. "Just as soon as she sniffs that wool and decides it's her own lamb. And she makes it a real good mother, too. Yes sir, I think it would be good for Boss to have a bum lamb now."

He drew on his pipe and took a swallow of hot coffee. "You stay here with Boss for a while if she'll let you, hear? But don't tell her I said so. Ever since Ben was killed, she don't take kindly to people figurin' out what she should do."

"Who's Ben?"

Tex didn't answer for a few minutes. He teetered back on the bench and his eyes looked far off. He seemed to be making up his mind. Finally he decided and he leaned forward.

"I'm goin' to tell you about Boss so you'll understand her a little better. She won't tell you, that is for sure. She don't talk much and never about herself. Maybe later on she'll get around to

36

explaining to you about Ben, but I think you should know now. Don't you tell her that I've been talkin' about her." He finished the mug of coffee and rose to refill it. "Ben was her son. He was killed by a grizzly, a bear, two winters back when he was out huntin'. Boss spent a whole year lookin' for that bear and never did find it. There was never anyone in the world like Ben to her. Sometimes I think that's why she took old Bezeleel's place here when he got bit, just so she could be out here and find that bear. Angie said she should try to hire a herder but she wouldn't listen. These ewes in her flock are the best on the ranch, the real money-makers, so it's a special job and Boss decided to do it herself."

The boy was confused. "Who's Angie?"

"Ben's wife, Ben's widow now. She lives on the ranch and teaches school in town. Angie got real upset about Boss comin' way out here alone with the sheep for the winter. That's what I mean by sayin' Boss don't take kindly to people tellin' her what she should do. The more Angie talked, the stubborner Boss got, and I ain't never seen anyone could beat her at bein' stubborn." He slapped his leg. "There I go again. One thing Angie can't stand, bein' a schoolteacher, is someone saying ain't. I been trying tryin' my best to get over it but it slipped out again."

The boy wanted to hear the rest of the story.

"Did you think Boss should have come out here?"

Tex whooped with laughter. "Me? I'm only a hired hand for now. I kept out of it. I'm just here to tend the camps of the herders and to do chores around the ranch. But some day . . ."

His eyes looked far off again. He reminded the boy of how the old man had looked driving down the highways. As though there was something beautiful way past the next hill that no one else could see.

"Some day," Tex said, "I'm goin' to have me a sheep ranch, too. Sheep as far as you can see, dottin' the hills all around my ranch." He slapped his leg again and stood up. "I've talked enough for one day. Got to go now. I'll bring the food and kerosene in and lay the wood under the wagon." He moved toward the door.

"You still a loner?" the boy asked.

A grin spread over Tex's face. "I been gettin' over it lately, that's how come I gave you all that good advice. You better get over it, too." He winked. "You put up with Boss as long as she'll have you. When she does talk, you'll hear a lot about Ben and about the bear and about sheep, but I reckon you can stand that. Seems to me you two belong together, a nice old ewe and a bum lamb." He threw up his hands and let out a loud whoop. "Don't tell her I said that, though. She'd skin me alive for callin' her an old ewe." He left, laughing.

When Tex finished his chores, the boy watched him walk down the hill and get into the provision truck. He watched until the truck disappeared down the road between the cottonwoods and the quaking aspens and willows.

The boy thought about Ben and Boss, the bear, and Angie, and Tex for a long time. Tex had advised him to stay here if he could. It made sense. If he kept wandering around the country alone, some day someone would find out he didn't belong anywhere and they'd put him in one of those homes Tex had grown up in. Women who came to visit the pickers' camps were always threatening to put the children in homes somewhere. They said the children ought to be where they could go to school regularly and live like other people. Well, he'd had too much freedom in his life to like the idea of that. Maybe Tex was right. If Boss would have him he'd like to stay here for a while, maybe until next spring.

He began to study how to make Boss want him to stay. He remembered how she'd made him wash last night. That must mean that she liked for people to be clean. All right, if he had to be clean to stay, then he'd get used to it. Finding the pan he had washed in before, he poured water into it from the bucket. The water was warm from standing near the stove so he used it as it was. He stripped off the nightshirt and dropped the soap into the pan. Then, with the end of the towel, he washed himself thoroughly, better than he ever had in his life. Some of the crop-pickers had had portable tubs and he had seen them bathing on Saturday nights, in the middle of their shacks, the whole family waiting in line for their turn. No one he had ever traveled with had carried a tub. The ones he had known had left it up to each person to do what washing he wanted to at the spigot that supplied the whole camp with water. There in the sheep wagon the boy used the towel to dry himself and put his nightshirt back on again. He threw the water out the door as he had seen Boss do.

He ate another biscuit with beans and climbed back into bed. His body cried out for sleep and rest and he curled up under the blankets, grasping the bag of potatoes close to him, although the wagon was warm now. There was no way of knowing what time it was and, even if he had known, it wouldn't have mattered. Boss would be home at sundown. Until then he would sleep.

4

The boy awoke to sounds outside the wagon. He pulled himself up to the window and looked out. It was late afternoon and the golden haze he remembered from yesterday lay on the dry grass and the slopes near by. The sheep were slowly coming toward the bed ground, grazing as they moved forward. The reflection of the sky tinted their wool, and to the boy they looked like a floating golden cloud lying soft above the ground as far as he could see. Boss wasn't in sight but he saw a dog working one side of the band. It ran up and down on the outer edge of the flock, guiding, directing the sheep toward the bed ground. This must be one of the dogs Tex had talked about. He saw it go after one sheep that had strayed a little way off from the others. Taking it gently by the ear, the big black-and-white dog led it back to the others, left it there, and went on with his work.

He heard a low-pitched whistle and then saw

another dog, smaller, and all white except for dark brown ears, appear from the other side, working the sheep to the right so that they headed toward the bed ground where the flags marked off the borders.

Boss opened the door a few minutes later, pulling her hat off and running her hands through her short hair as she entered the wagon. "Been all right today?" she asked. Her gaze was so sharp that he felt she knew at once he had bathed, but she didn't say anything about it. He nodded, surprised again at her size.

She saw the new supplies and the mail. "Tex been here?"

The boy nodded again. "He said to tell you weather was coming so he brought things out today. And that the old man's dog that bit him was sick. He called it something else but I can't remember what."

Boss nodded. "I figured that." She had pulled her coat off and was getting ready to mix food in two bowls. "Sometimes I wonder if I did wrong, not having all the dogs we own given that vaccine for rabies." She seemed to be talking to herself. "But Ben was so dead set against it after Jup's father died from the shot." She realized the boy was there. "What else did Tex say?"

"Nothing much." He remembered Tex's warning not to let her know they had spent most of the time talking about her.

"He's a good worker but a big talker. If he didn't say more than that he must be off his feed." The boy said nothing and Boss didn't press the matter. She finished mixing the food. "I'm going out and feed the dogs and count the sheep," she said. "Then I'll come in and clean up and get us some supper."

The boy looked at her, round-eyed. "You know enough numbers to count all of them?" he asked. To him the sheep were endless, covering the ground all around the wagon.

She laughed and drew him to the window. "Look out there. You'll see some black sheep among the rest. They're the ones I count. There's one of them for every hundred white — and we call them markers. If all nine are there, it's safe to figure we haven't lost any."

She left the wagon with the bowls and the boy stayed at the window and looked out. He counted the number of black sheep he saw. There were only six but he couldn't see all the flock. He couldn't see Boss or the dogs either, but he guessed she was feeding them right outside the wagon. He stayed there, staring at the sheep. Some were slowly grazing their way to the bed ground on the slant between the flags, while others had already kneeled and found a place for the night. He saw with surprise that their fleece was gray and greasy-looking now that the sunlight had gone. Their legs looked too thin for their bodies and they seemed to be standing on the tips of their small split hooves. Tears spilled from their eyes. Now and then they raised their heads and blatted sadly, their cleft upper lips quivering.

After a while Boss came back into the wagon. "No wind tonight," she said, "though it may blow up later if weather's coming. That's the biggest worry I have, along with coyotes."

"Wind don't blow them away, does it?" the boy asked, still thinking of them as they had looked in the golden light — like a cloud, soft and airy.

Boss looked at him quickly to see if he was joking.

"No, though it does seem to blow their wits away. A sheep doesn't like to feel its wool ruffled so it's just as apt to get up and walk into the wind. And if one goes, they all go."

The boy thought about that. "Guess they're pretty dumb, huh?"

Boss whirled on him. "Dumb? They're not dumb. They're just about the most helpless creatures alive. They've lost all their instinct to take care of themselves because they haven't had to. But it isn't their fault. It's man's. He's bred all the wild animal's independence and cunning out of them for his own gain, to have their meat and their wool with the least possible bother from them. Don't ever use that word about them again in my hearing. I won't have it!"

44

She stood there, red-faced with anger, and the boy swallowed hard. He wasn't off to a very good start at making her like him and want him to stay. It was a new game to him and he realized he wasn't very good at it. But if he wanted to stay enough, he could learn how to think of what she'd like before he did or said anything.

Slowly her face relaxed. "I know people call them stupid. They say they're the only animals alive that are born determined to get themselves killed one way or another as soon as possible. But I happen to love those sheep, every one of them, and Ben did, too. He spent his time caring for them from the time he was just a child. He kept them from straying off and getting lost, kept them out of the coyotes' way, kept them from eating the locoweed that drives them crazy. I know they seem to be bent on doing things that will destroy them, but that's the reason I'm here. To keep them safe, to keep them together."

The boy turned his face to the wall while Boss washed herself and changed her clothes. Evening had come and the sheep had settled down. The wagon was warm and comfortable and the deep weariness of his body was almost gone. He thought about what Boss had said. It surprised him to hear her talk like that about sheep. People he'd known spent their time taking care of themselves. Boss took care of sheep.

She pulled the table up and propped it with the folding leg. They ate stewed tomatoes and scrambled eggs and some of the biscuits left over from morning. She opened a glass of blackberry jelly and spread it on the biscuits, and poured a cup of half canned milk and half water for the boy.

"Why didn't you drink some today?" she asked. "Didn't you see the note I left telling you it was on the ledge outside to keep cool?"

He didn't say anything. Raidy had placed such store on reading and writing, maybe Boss did, too. He hadn't even guessed the note was for him. If he said he couldn't read, she might think he ought to go to school and learn. And that would probably mean he would have to live in one of those children's homes. He had to be very careful before he said anything.

Boss watched his face and he was sure she knew what he was thinking. Without saying anything she cleared away the dishes, then brought her boots and a jar of grease to the table. She worked the grease into the leather with her fingers and wiped it off with a cloth. Her large hands were rough but the nails were evenly trimmed and clean. "Ben cleaned his boots every night of his life," she said. "I never had to tell him to do it."

The boy was glad he had bathed. It had been the right thing to do, something Ben would have done without being told.

When she finished, she put the boots on the floor

and went to the long bench. Inside it she found a book and brought it back to the table.

"I've been thinking all day about a name," she said. "Seems to me you ought to pick one out for yourself. There's a lot of fine names in the Bible here."

The boy knew what the Bible was. There had been men who came to the pickers' camps on Sundays, and read out of the Bible to anyone who would listen.

"I decided the best way was to let you hold the Bible and turn to wherever you want. Then put your finger on the page and we'll see what it says."

He took the book and held it between his hands. The cover was of smooth leather and there were gold letters across the front of it. He hesitated, thinking of Raidy. He wished she could be here now to see him get a name, his own name.

Opening the book he pressed the pages flat on his knees. Then he placed his finger on a place and held it there. Boss covered his finger with her large one and took the book. For a minute she didn't say anything.

The boy couldn't stand the waiting. "What does it say?" he asked.

Her voice was very low. "You turned to First Samuel, chapter sixteen. And put your finger on these words, 'Send me David thy son, which is with the sheep!' "

"That mean my name is David?"

She shut the book slowly. "It's a fine name . . ."

He was curious. "Who was he?"

"A shepherd," Boss said. "A very brave and loyal shepherd. When he was only a boy in charge of his father's flock, he risked his life to protect his sheep."

"How?" The boy wanted to know all there was to know about this David whose name he would be taking.

"One day when the sheep were grazing, a hungry lion snatched one out of the flock and ran off with it. David went after him and took the sheep right out of his mouth. The lion turned on him then and David killed it with his bare hands."

"Wow! He sure was brave, wasn't he?"

Boss nodded. "He was. But what I like best about the story is that he didn't stop to think about the danger when one of his sheep was gone. They were in his care and he knew he had to protect them. That's what a shepherd's for, to look out for his sheep even if it means risking his own life. You could be very proud of a name like that but you'd also have a lot to live up to."

She rose and put the book away. "Get into bed. This one." She was pointing to the one on the bench. "You'll use it after this — David."

He lay in bed thinking about his name, trying it over and over until it began to sound familiar on his tongue. Somewhere, long ago, there had been a David who had taken care of sheep, and now he was going to use that name, too. He curled up under the sugan and thought sleepily that it was strange how he had picked out a shepherd's name.

He heard the dogs barking in the night, and then was aware that Boss was leaving the wagon. He got up and watched out the window while she built a fire, and saw by its light the sheep huddled close together. Far off he heard a weird high-pitched howl. The dogs stood alert at the edge of the flock and Boss walked around the bed ground, a flaming stick in her hand. He lay down again, determined to stay awake and find out what had happened when Boss came back to bed, but the next thing he knew it was morning and she and the sheep and the dogs were gone.

David had eaten breakfast and was standing with his face pressed against the panes of the door window when he saw a small car appear on the road through the trees at the foot of the hill. He watched as it stopped and saw a girl get out. For one wild, crazy, endless minute he thought it was Raidy. The sun that sifted through the cotton-woods fell on her hair and he saw that it was yellow and tied behind her head. From the distance she seemed to be Raidy's size, but she wore trousers and boots and a red shirt under her sheepskin coat. The only clothes Raidy had owned had been a thin dress and a ragged sweater. He watched as she took a large package from the car and carried it toward the wagon. Numb with shock, he saw she was bigger than Raidy had been, and older. He had known it couldn't be Raidy, and the wild joy that had leaped up in him when he first saw her left him and he backed away to the bed at the end of the wagon and sat on it, waiting.

She opened the door of the wagon and stood there. Her quick smile was like Raidy's but her eyes were brown instead of blue, and he could see that she was a woman, not a girl.

"Hello," she said. "May I come in?"

He nodded and slid farther back on the bed.

She laid the package on the bench and unbuttoned her coat. "I'm Angie," she said. "Tex told me about you. I figured you might need some warm clothes with the weather turning cold so I packed some up and brought them out."

He didn't say anything, only watched as she filled the coffeepot and set it on the stove.

"All those clothes of Ben's up in the attic," she went on. "I don't think Boss ever threw anything away in her life. She's got trunks and trunks of things up there. And old things all over the ranch. Old guns in the blacksmith's shop, and harnesses and bridles hung on the walls of the barn, and even an old sleigh that no one has used for years. And bear traps by the dozen — "

David edged forward. "Bear traps?"

"Sure," she said, turning toward him, her long hair swinging across her shoulder and back again, just the way Raidy's used to do. "She's always setting bear traps. Got them all over the woods around here. Oh, it's safe enough. Nobody uses these woods in the winter."

"What are they like?" he asked. "I ain't — " he remembered what Tex had said about her not liking that word " — I never seen one."

"Oh, jaw traps mostly, I guess. The kind with a pan in between that works a lever when the animal steps on it. I've never paid much attention but Boss could tell you all about them."

When the coffee was done, she poured herself a cup and brought it over to the bench. "Nice and warm in here," she said, leaning back and crossing her legs in front of her. "What's your name? That Tex told me he didn't even think to ask you!"

He remembered then that he had a name. "David," he said. He said it again — "It's David."

"Then you're in the right place. I suppose you know David in the Bible was a shepherd?"

"Sure," the boy said. "I was named after him."

He liked Angie. Maybe he liked her because she looked like Raidy, maybe because she had brought the clothes all the way from the ranch for him. Or maybe because she knew how to break the strangeness between them by talking about bear traps.

"First time you've been in Montana?" She didn't ask why are you here or where did you come from.

"Yes." For the first time he felt like talking about the crop-picking and the potato-digging machine and about what happened to Raidy. But he didn't. Some day he would tell her; he was sure of that. But not yet.

She picked up the package and began to open it. As she laid the clothes in piles, she told him, "I was a schoolteacher before I married Ben and I went back to teaching again, afterward." She didn't say after what but he had the feeling she knew Tex had told him about Ben.

She held up a pair of trousers and a flannel shirt. "These look as if they might fit. And here's some underwear and a pair of boots." She laughed. "You know what Tex said when I asked him what size you were? He said 'He's little but mighty. Give him a chance and he'll end up tall and strong as a young cottonwood.' So from that I had to guess what would fit."

David was pleased. He picked up a sheepskin coat and a cap and a pair of wool-lined gloves. He could wear these when Boss let him go outside again.

"Now," Angie said, looking at him critically, "let's trim your hair. We'll give Boss a real surprise when she gets home."

When they finished, they ate biscuits and beans and cold tomatoes, and Angie showed him how to do things around the wagon. She showed him how the stove worked, how to wash the dishes, where the broom was kept, and how to sweep out the wagon. She took him to the window and pointed out the direction of the creek. "You can get water there. And be a big help to Boss by doing the chores around here."

She moved back to the table. "I'd like to leave a note for Boss if you can find a pencil and some paper." David found them on top of a shelf and Angie wrote almost a page in fine small writing. He watched her. It looked so easy and she did it so much faster than Raidy. The letters flowed delicate and slender and straight from her pencil.

"Will you show me how to write my name?" he asked.

She took a fresh piece of paper and wrote it slowly. "Study it, and write it yourself, and the next time I come I'll begin teaching you the letters and how to write them." She had guessed he had never been to school.

"Will you do me a favor?" he asked. "Will you read me about the other David in the Bible? I know where Boss keeps it."

"I'd rather tell you about him," she said, "about David with the sheep." She told him how David, who was only a young boy and a shepherd, had seen a lion and a bear take a lamb from the flock. The boy went in pursuit and hit out, forcing lion and bear to drop the lamb. Then when the attack turned on him, David seized the lion by the beard, struck and killed him. The shepherd boy killed both the lion and the bear and saved his father's lamb.

The boy sighed when she finished. "I guess there aren't any more adventures like that. I'd like to try to do what David did."

"I hope there aren't," she said. "A lion and a bear — even though the bears were smaller than the ones around here — well!"

He whistled. "Oh boy," he said, "that David sure was brave, wasn't he? I bet not many people would dare to face such odds."

Angie got up and put on her coat. "Lots of things in your life can seem pretty overwhelming, David. It's not being afraid to try to conquer them that counts . . . it's having the faith and courage that shepherd boy had when he accepted the challenge. I'm sure you have that courage."

After she was gone, he tried on the clothes. They were only a little too big.

5

When Boss came into the wagon at sundown and saw him wearing Ben's clothes, she stopped still and put her hand over her heart. Her large body sagged and she put out her other hand to steady herself against the stove. Her sharp blue eyes clouded and her mouth straightened into a thin line.

The boy stood there, sensing the shock it had been to her. He watched her face. "She doesn't like me wearing Ben's clothes," he thought. "She wishes it were Ben here instead of me, just like I wished Angie was Raidy today."

He took the note Angie had left and gave it to Boss. She sat down heavily on the bench and read it. She was quiet so long that David turned and went to the window and looked out at the sheep grazing near the bed ground.

Finally she spoke. "As long as you're dressed, you might as well come outside with me." She didn't say anything about what was in the note. Taking two bowls, she filled them with food.

David stood on the steps of the wagon, breathing the sharp cold air that cut like a knife into his lungs. The dogs were eating and he skirted them widely as he went past. The only dogs he had known had been the snarling half-wild ones that hung around the pickers' camps, stealing what food they could. All the camp children had considered them enemies and had driven them away with rocks and sticks. Only Raidy had loved them, just as she had loved everything homeless and alone.

"Come on," Boss said, and led him to the edge of the flock. The sheep raised their heads as he approached, looking at him curiously. Then the ones nearest him began to stamp their feet.

"Stand still," Boss said, "and let them get used to you. Anything they're not used to excites them."

David stood still, eying the sheep that kept up their stamping. Only one, an old ewe, came to the boy and stood beside him, her tear-filled eyes watching him.

"Who's that?" he asked, pointing at her.

Boss looked at the ewe fondly. "That's Cluny. She's one of the oldest sheep in the flock, a good breeder and her wool is the very best. She was Ben's pet, hardly ever left his side."

The ewe, her widespread teeth showing her age, nuzzled his arm. "She wants to be friends with me," David said. "She's not like the rest of them."

Boss smiled. "You're right about that. Cluny is the exception to all rules about sheep. They say all sheep are timid. Not Cluny. I don't believe she's ever been afraid of anything in her life. They say a sheep that acts different from the rest of the flock is a sick sheep. Why, Cluny's been doing things her own way since the day she was born. They say a flock has one mind, that they all do what the leader does. Well, this flock has two minds — Cluny's and the other nine hundred's. Most anybody who had a sheep like that in a flock would figure it to be a leader. Not Cluny. She'd rather wander off by herself and investigate things. She won't put up with other sheep following her, just waits her time and then disappears if she feels like exploring. She drives Jup wild but he loves her. He's always watching out for her."

"I like her, too," David said, rubbing his hands through her matted wool. "I like her because she's a loner," he thought, "and because I know how she feels."

After a while the sheep stopped stamping and slowly crowded forward, convinced the stranger wouldn't harm them, curious to examine him more closely.

"Count the markers for me," Boss said, busy straightening the flags.

There were nine markers present. "Did you build the fire because of coyotes last night? Was that why the dogs barked?" he asked.

Boss nodded. "They were hanging around last night. Mean, ornery critters, but they're smart. They've got a lot of respect for man, though. That's why I lighted the fire. Fire to them means man. When you're up against coyotes you have to use every trick you can think of because they're the most cunning, the slipperiest, the speediest smart alecks on these plains and they'll eat anything they can find. They like sheep best, though."

Jup and Juno came up, sniffing David's legs and looking up at him. He backed away, his fingers itching to pick up a rock. Jup seemed to feel his dislike immediately and backed off, his eyes clear and bright and curious, fixed on the boy's face. Juno stayed near.

"Notice Jup's eyes," Boss said over her shoulder. "He's got what is known as the eagle look. It can hypnotize a sheep and make her do exactly what he wants her to. Ben noticed it first when Jup was about four months old. That puppy would round up all the chickens in the ranch yard and herd them into the barn. He did it over and over again until I thought he'd wear them out. He's been a working dog ever since he was born. Never had time for puppy romping. That's why Ben wouldn't have any other dog but Jup when he was out with a flock."

David looked at the big black-and-white collie. This had been Ben's dog. If Ben were standing here now, what would he do? Reach out and pat the dog's head probably. From the way Boss talked, everything Ben had done had been the right thing to do, the way Ben had done it, the right way.

He reached out a hand toward Jup but the dog backed away and sat down, still looking at him. Juno, the white collie, leaped up, wagging her tail. She was easy to make friends with. The boy had a feeling Jup knew why he was offering his friendship and it wasn't good enough. He sat there, tall for a dog, deep-chested, aloof. His fine head was tilted to one side and his eyes were questioning.

Boss watched and frowned. As a rule Jup was friendly, almost too friendly sometimes for a good sheep dog. It was as much his job to protect the flock from strangers as it was to guard it from coyotes. This wasn't like him.

In the distance the staccato yip-yap of a coyote pierced the air and immediately both dogs came to full alert. The yaps were followed by long howls and it was impossible to tell whether the cries were made by one animal or half a dozen. The cry was menacing and David shivered as he listened.

59

A restless wave passed over the bedded-down sheep, and they shifted position so that their faces were turned inward toward the bed ground, their throats away from the danger of snarling, snapping jaws. Only Cluny lay at the edge of the flock, unafraid.

"Looks like another long night," Boss said. "Let's build a fire, then go in and have dinner." David brought wood from under the wagon and watched as Boss stacked and set fire to it. The sheep huddled together, and mysterious shadows appeared in the flickering light. Both dogs stood tense at the edge of the flock, their ears raised and their noses sniffing the air.

While they were eating, David offered to help stand guard that night. He wanted to carry a lighted torch the way Boss had done. Tex had said maybe it was time he tried to help someone else. "I could take a turn while you slept."

She shook her head. "Jup isn't sure of you. I can't leave the flock in your charge because it would worry him. You had best get your sleep. I'd like to see you strong, with a little more meat on your bones, before we make plans for you."

She left the washing up of the dishes to him and put on her heavy jacket, the old felt hat, the wool-lined gloves, before going outside.

David lay in bed and thought about what had happened. Everything had gone wrong. He remembered Boss's face when she saw him dressed in Ben's clothes. Her words — "Jup isn't sure of you . . . before we make plans for you" — didn't sound as if she meant to have him stay. If she'd given him a chance to guard the flock tonight, Jup would have gotten used to him. If she meant him to stay, what kind of plans did she need to make?

Maybe she didn't want anyone taking Ben's place with her. Maybe she was the ewe that didn't want a bum lamb. Even with Ben's clothes on, like the skin they put on the bum lamb to fool the ewe, she wouldn't have him. It all added up to one thing in his mind. He didn't belong in the sheep wagon and he'd better be getting on to California fast. What was he doing here anyway? He was a loner and a loner took care of himself. He wouldn't ever change, no matter what Tex said.

Angie would get him started. She would give him some food and show him which way to go. Maybe she'd be disappointed because the plan she and Tex had of having him stay with Boss hadn't worked out, but she'd understand. The ranch was somewhere up the road through the trees, maybe four or five miles. He'd just follow that. He could wait till Tex came out next week with the provisions but that was merely putting it off. If he was going to get out of these mountains before the snows came, he'd better be starting.

"I don't need anyone to take care of me," he

told himself. "I can take care of myself." He snuggled down in the warm bed. He would miss all of this, miss the food Boss cooked, even Boss herself. But he didn't blame her. Nobody but Raidy had ever really wanted him to stay. Most folks didn't want a stray around.

6

Boss started the sheep home early from the grazing area. Light snow had fallen during the last two hours and the sky promised more before long. She was tired. For two nights now she had spent most of the hours between sunset and sunrise on watch for coyotes. She had taken a bedroll outside and put it by the fire, getting up when the dogs grew restless or when the fire needed tending.

Her body ached with weariness. "Maybe Angie's right," she thought. "Maybe I am too old to be out here, doing a man's work. This crazy notion of mine about finding the bear that killed Ben!" So far she hadn't seen a sign of bear. She had traps in the woods and she kept a sharp lookout for tracks every day, but she had seen nothing at all.

She thought about David. It had been better out here on the range and in the sheep wagon since he had come. It gave her something to think about during the long days with the sheep. He didn't look like Ben as a boy, yet it had taken her breath away when she had walked into the wagon and found him dressed in Ben's clothes. Such a lot of memories had rushed at her during that moment that she had been forced to sit down and get hold of herself. Ben was gone, gone for good. For two years now she had been telling herself this, over and over. Then, almost like a miracle, the boy had appeared.

She wished she had Angie's way of showing what she felt. If only she could be as gentle and kind as Angie! She had never been able to speak her feelings, not even to Ben. But Ben had known her as well as she knew herself. He had guessed that all her life her bigness had set her apart from other women, from the softness and the tenderness everyone expected from women. She had developed a man's way of showing affection, not in words but in actions. Words just didn't come easy to her.

For instance, when the boy had stared at her there in the sheep wagon while she felt the shock of seeing him in Ben's clothes, why hadn't she said to him, "It's all right. Just give me a minute to get used to it. I'm glad to have you wearing Ben's clothes, glad I kept them." And why didn't she tell him last night when he offered to guard the sheep for her, "Give Jup some time to get to know you. Give me time to teach you about sheepherding. There's so much to learn."

The sheep approached a narrow aisle between two bronze hills and she whistled to the dogs, telling them to turn the band to the left as they came out of the small pass. Jup nipped at the heels of the lead sheep, urging it on so there would be no chance of a pile-up. It was times like this when the lead sheep could move too slowly, or run into a barrier, that the hundreds of other ewes behind her would keep on coming, piling the sheep into a mass of smothering, dying animals as the trampling went on and on. It could happen with lightning speed and was the worst of all the dangers threatening the sheep.

She drove the sheep over the last hill before the one the wagon stood on. Rose-colored rock cliffs hung above the meadow on one side, and on the other, along the bank of the stream, stood quaking aspen trees, their golden leaves almost gone now. The light snow clung to their branches and glistened in the late afternoon glow.

She saw smoke curling from the chimney of the wagon as she came down the hill and thought how long the days must seem to the boy who waited there. Angie's note had told her briefly what Tex had learned of the boy's life, that he was entirely alone. She had thought of sending him to the ranch

65

and letting Angie start him in school, but she felt he wasn't ready for that yet. Let him stay with her through the winter and spring. Then he could have the summer on the ranch, and begin school in the fall. In the meantime she would take him with her and begin to teach him how to handle the flock. When he had picked the name of David out of the Bible, it had been almost like a sign to her that he belonged with her, with the sheep. It would be good for him to have a winter on the range while she fattened him up along with the sheep. And good for her, too, to fill the emptiness of her life out here.

The wagon was vacant when Boss opened the door. The beds were made, the floor swept, and the breakfast dishes had been washed and put away in the cupboard. She stood there, puzzled, for a few minutes, then turned and, standing on the steps, studied the surrounding area. There was no sign of the boy. Thinking he might be down at the stream, she called his name. The dogs came to the wagon, looking up at her curiously. There was no answer.

She went inside the wagon and looked around. The cap and sheepskin jacket were gone. Then she saw that the sugan which usually lay on his bed wasn't there. She checked things quickly. He had taken a box of matches from beside the stove, and the biscuit pan was empty. She knew then he had left and she felt anger rising in her. Why? Hadn't he liked it here? Certainly it was better than the miserable life he had led picking crops. Or was it her fault? She had never even told him she wanted him to stay.

It was getting dark now and she knew it would be dangerous for him to wander about the mountains at night. I'll go after him, she decided. Then if he really doesn't like it here, if he wants to leave, she and Angie would arrange it somehow.

She called Juno into the wagon, waving Jup back to the sheep. Juno's delight at being allowed in the wagon was plain to see. She went from place to place, sniffing and prancing with excitement. Boss took Bezeleel's old nightshirt and showed it to Juno. "We've got to find him," she said. "Where did he go?" Juno sniffed the shirt for a long time, whining softly and nuzzling it with her nose.

Boss took a flashlight and called to Jup, "Stay with the sheep. We'll be back soon." She carried the nightshirt over her arm and showed it again to Juno. "Which way did he go? Which way, girl?"

Juno danced around the wagon, her nose just above the ground. At last she snuffled loudly and led the way down the hill toward the road. Boss followed her. They went through the trees and along the winding road that led back to the ranch. Once out of the woods, the road cut across a small plain and then wound steeply up a hill. Juno led

67

the way, stopping now and then to make certain she was on the right path, then bounding ahead out of sight. It was beginning to grow dark and Boss flicked on the flashlight, the spot of light skipping ahead of her through the dark.

These hills and mountains were tricky. The rocky walls that looked so solid from a distance were often honeycombed and could break away at the weight of a foot. There were abandoned mines all around and even open pits in some places. Ben had known these mountains so well! He had often hunted in them, telling her about the occasional cougar or wolf or bear he had seen. For the thousandth time she thought about the bear that had killed Ben. Had Ben come upon him in the midst of a kill when a bear was the most dangerous? Had the bear been wounded by someone else and waited there in the brush to attack when Ben came by? Had Ben, while out on that hunt, caught him on a raid and failed to hit a vital spot so that the bear had charged before Ben could get off another shot? She'd never know the answer, but if that grizzly ever crossed her path it would pay for Ben's death.

She and Juno saw the fire flickering through the brush at the same time. Juno raced forward and up the incline off the road. Boss was right behind her, scrambling, pulling herself up over the rocks that clung to the side of the mountain.

"Wait," she called softly to the dog. She moved

forward quietly. Through the trees she saw the small fire and beyond it the mouth of a cave. The boy sat there, wrapped in the sugan, his face lighted by the fire. His knees were drawn up and his arms around them. Juno stayed beside Boss, obediently, but her body wriggled with joy.

Boss bit her lip. It was the loneliest sight she had ever seen, the small figure surrounded by the immense darkness. Her heart went out to the boy. He had plenty of courage, enough for ten boys his size.

David went back with Boss and Juno willingly. He was so glad to see them he didn't even think of his plans for going on to California. Boss hadn't found the words to tell him how worried she had been when she found him gone or how much she wanted him back. "He'll know because I came after him," she thought. Why did everything always have to be put into words? She didn't realize that the boy was too new at having a home to suspect how she felt or that he couldn't allow himself to take anything for granted yet.

David was glad she had come. He had been surprised because he thought she'd wanted to be rid of him. It had been lonely in the mountains, in the dark. He had huddled beside the fire, wondering what was going on in the strange land around him.

"How would you feel," Boss said, "if a thousand-pound grizzly came home and found you'd moved into his cave? Or if a cougar happened by and decided a boy would take the place of the deer he hadn't been able to find for his dinner? These things can happen here, David. You've got to use common sense when you live in this country. You can't take chances."

She carried the nightshirt and the sugan and let him take the flashlight. Juno danced at his side, happy to have him back, happy to have found him. He played the flashlight on the path ahead, watching it skip along the uneven ground and stab through the night.

They were going through the trees toward the wagon when they heard it. The snarls and yips were faint, but even from this distance Boss knew what was happening. "It's Jup," she cried. "The coyotes are after him." Juno flashed ahead, a white streak, and Boss started after her. For all her bigness, she could move fast and it was hard for David to keep up.

They found the bed ground in confusion. Sheep pushed against one another, milling around in terror. David shone the flashlight beyond the flags. Jup lay on the ground, blood staining his rough coat and soft whimpering sounds coming from his throat. The coyotes were gone, but a trail of blood showed they, too, had suffered in the battle.

Boss kneeled beside Jup, her fingers running

70

over his body. "He's got some bad wounds," she said, "but they'll heal. All I hope is those coyotes weren't rabid."

She took the flashlight and made a quick tour of the bed ground. Now the sheep were spread out, the flock in a panic, going off in all directions. She whistled and Juno began immediately rounding up the band and heading them back toward the bed ground. Jup heard the whistle and raised his head, his forefeet attempting to grip the earth and raise himself up — but his strength was gone and he fell back. "Lie still, Jup," Boss commanded.

"David, build a fire. I'm going after the sheep that have strayed. Take care of Jup. The coyotes must have ganged up on him but I don't think they'll be back tonight. Not after the punishment he must have given them. They're probably now in their dens, licking their wounds." She and Juno disappeared in the dark.

The boy carried wood from the wagon and built a fire near the bed ground. Then he went to where Jup lay and looked down at him. Cluny had come to lie beside him. She hadn't panicked. She acted as if an attack by coyotes was an everyday occurrence. What did Boss expect him to do for the dog? He couldn't lift him and carry him to the fire. Jup was too heavy. That's what Ben would probably have done, but Ben had been a strong man.

How did you take care of someone? When he

71

himself had been sick in that shack in Florida, the man and woman had covered him with a blanket and left him some water. He found the sugan that had been dropped by the wagon in the excitement and carried it to where Jup lay. Then he took a cloth and dipped it in the water bucket, squeezed it, and held it to the dog's mouth. Jup lapped at it thirstily and David went back to the bucket three times. Reaching out, he stroked the dog's head and saw that under the sugan the dog's tail was moving faintly. He was surprised that he was no longer afraid of Jup. For the first time in his life, someone really needed him.

He lighted a torch and circled the flock as Boss had done, returning to Jup after each trip. There were no sounds of coyotes, no sign of them. Cluny lay beside Jup, her eyes regarding him steadily. About an hour before dawn, Boss returned, driving about fifty sheep ahead of her. David was asleep, curled between Cluny and Jup. The tired ewes made for the bed ground and settled down, and Boss awakened the boy.

"Take the sugan and lay it on the floor of the wagon," she said. "I'll carry Jup inside." Gently she lifted the big dog in her arms. When they had him settled and had washed his wounds and painted them with medicine, she motioned to the boy.

"Let's check to see how many the coyotes got."

They went back to where Jup had been, then on beyond toward the stream. There they found three ewes, their throats torn out.

"Those coyotes are smart," Boss said angrily, looking down at the dead sheep. "They ganged up on Jup and, while he was busy fighting them, some of the rest dragged these ewes off. They knew he was alone. That's why two dogs are best. A gang-up is too much for one dog to handle."

David knew that if Boss and Juno hadn't had to come after him, Jup wouldn't have been alone. And there would have been a fire to scare the coyotes away. He felt miserable, as though he had killed the ewes himself. Kneeling down beside one, he touched her greasy gray wool. "The only good thing about it," he thought, "is that they didn't get Cluny."

Boss skinned the sheep, her mouth a hard line. By the time they got back to the wagon, the sheep were stirring on the bed ground and light had begun to streak through the darkness.

7

For the next two weeks, David's job was taking care of Jup. He and Boss made the dog a bed on the floor of the wagon and the boy saw to it that Jup lay on it quietly. When the sheep stirred in the early morning, Jup would whine and struggle to get up, but David was out of bed and beside him instantly, talking to him and holding him down. When Boss brought the flock back in the evening, it took all David's strength to convince Jup he wasn't needed outside. The eagle eyes of the dog were alert as his ears followed the sounds of every movement of the sheep. As his wounds healed, he grew restless and several times David let him stand on Boss's bed, his paws on the window, waiting for the sheep to come home. It was a new experience for the boy, taking care of someone else. He put his whole heart into it, partly to make up for causing the trouble in the first place, partly because he was growing to understand and love the dog.

When Boss read from her Bible he could not get enough of hearing about David the shepherd. They had read many of his adventures by now — all about Goliath.

Angie came on Saturdays when school was not in session, and she and David worked on the alphabet, on the lessons she brought from her school class.

At the end of two weeks, Boss pronounced Jup recovered. "It's too soon to tell about rabies," she said, "but we'll watch him and if he shows no signs in another two weeks, we can stop worrying."

"What kind of signs?" the boy asked.

"Wildness, a change in the way he behaves, a change in his appetite, snapping at things."

"What would you do if he acted that way?"

Without hesitating, Boss said, "Shoot him."

David gave a cry and stared at her. "Shoot Jup?" The idea was so terrible he backed away from her and sat down. It couldn't happen. He stared at Boss accusingly.

"Would Ben have shot Jup if he had rabies? You said he loved him."

Boss nodded. "If Jup were sick it would be the kindest thing to do. And, too, the whole flock would be in danger, as well as you and I. That's the last thing Ben would have wanted. He knew that no matter how much you may love something, your duty comes first, and everything else has to come after that. A shepherd's first duty is to his flock."

When the meadows within a three-mile area were in danger of being overgrazed, Tex moved the sheep wagon. He brought two strong horses and hitched them to it and they pulled the wagon four miles nearer the mountains.

The new location was exciting to David because it was on a part of the range he hadn't seen before. On the south side of a hill nearby was a large roofed corral with many pens, and beside it were two small buildings.

"What are those?" he asked Tex.

"Cover for the sheep when the storms get too bad. The other two are storehouses for cottonseed cake and alfalfa hay and shelled corn. We brought it out here early in the fall. It's fed to the sheep when the range can't be used because of deep snow."

David explored the new range thoroughly. The bed ground was high on a spur with a sparse stand of tall timber about it. Close by was the stream, wider here and filled with icy crystal water, bubbling over dark rocks. Beyond the buildings on the other side of the wagon were willow trees with smooth polished bark, growing close together.

Peering into this small forest, David saw that it was dark and gloomy, growing more impenetrable the farther he looked.

The day after the wagon was moved, Boss declared a holiday and let the sheep graze close by. "Let them get used to this place," she said. She went on a tour of inspection of the buildings and the pens, then on to the forest of willows. David watched her studying the ground, going a short way into the trees and then back again. She walked the length of the meadow slowly, then hurried back to the sheep wagon. When she came out she was carrying a gun.

"I've found bear tracks. You and Jup take care of the sheep. I'll take Juno with me." She disappeared into the willows.

The boy climbed a high rock and sat down. He was in charge now, for the first time. He watched Jup, admiring the way the dog did his work, quietly but firmly controlling the sheep. David wanted Jup to know they were working together now so, whistling Boss's long low whistle, he waved his hand to let Jup know where he was.

To his surprise, Jup immediately leaped forward, rounding up the sheep, turning them toward the right, and driving them forward. The boy couldn't believe it. Was it possible that he had really given Jup a proper signal? He tried it again, whistling and waving his other hand. Jup backtracked at once around the flock and turned to the left. By this time the sheep were confused. They milled about, pressing against one another. His new power went to David's head and he whistled once more. The lead sheep started forward along a path beside a ravine. Suddenly all the sheep were following her, with Jup dashing wildly around the band, nipping their heels. Cluny headed off in another direction. Jup was after her immediately but Cluny refused to turn, her mind on some plan of her own. There was a tussle and desperately Jup grabbed the wool on her neck in his mouth and dragged her back toward the rest.

What would have happened if Boss hadn't appeared out of the woods just then, David dared not think. She saw quickly what was happening and called to Juno, "Head them off. Head them off." In a flash, the white dog was across the meadow and between the sheep and the ravine. Jup joined her there. Then, with a piercing whistle, Boss directed the dogs who turned the sheep around and back toward the pasture. In ten minutes the flock was grazing peacefully, as though nothing had happened.

Boss was out of breath. She had run the length of the meadow, David behind her. "What got into that crazy dog?" she panted. "I never saw him do anything like that before."

A plaintive blat came from the ravine and they

both ran to the edge. Ten feet below the path lay a fat ewe on her back, struggling. She lay helpless, looking up at them, her eyes brimming with tears. Boss and David climbed down the ravine together and hoisted her to her feet. They pushed and pulled her back to the path and watched her join the others, none the worse for her accident.

"Thank goodness she didn't break a leg. I'd have had to shoot her," Boss said. "What could that crazy Jup have been thinking of? In another few minutes all the flock would have been in that ravine, in the worst pile-up there could be."

She looked toward the meadow. There, between them and the sheep, was Jup. He was hunched over, coughing and snapping, his mouth opening and closing. His head bobbed back and forth, his body heaved and writhed. Something white hung from his jaws. Dragging himself around in a circle, he shook his head wildly.

David started to run to him but Boss shouted, "No!" She ran to where she had dropped her gun and raised it to her shoulder. David watched her take aim, then leaped between her and the dog.

"You can't!" he screamed. "You can't shoot him."

Boss's voice was harsh. "Don't go near that dog. He's having a fit. There's foam on his mouth. Get out of the way, David."

David paid no attention. He ran to Jup, carefully staying in a direct line between him and Boss. He kneeled beside the dog and caught his head between his hands. Jup was choking, a large string of white-gray wool hanging out of the side of his mouth. Holding Jup's jaws apart, David reached in and pulled out a ball of wool which had been caught in the dog's throat.

"There's nothing wrong with him but this," he called, holding up the wool. "It was stuck and he couldn't get it out."

Boss joined him. "I saw him pulling Cluny by the neck when the sheep started to scatter. That's probably when he got the wool in his mouth." The dog lay panting and David put his arms around him.

Boss was looking at Jup with unfriendly eyes. "Well, you saved his life, that's for sure. From back there I would have sworn he was foaming at the mouth. I thought he had rabies." She shook her head. "I can't understand why he panicked the sheep in the first place. I've left him in charge before but I guess I can't trust him any more." She turned and walked away.

David tried to call her back but he couldn't make a sound. He knew he should tell her it hadn't been Jup's fault. "I did it," he said to himself, "and she blames Jup. But I've got to look out for myself. With everything going so good I just can't ruin it now." He pressed his face against Jup's. "I can't tell her, Jup. I can't! Do you understand?" The dog struggled to his feet and nuzzled David's face. Then, recovered, he trotted away, back to his duty at the edge of the flock.

The rest of the day David stayed by himself. He took the books Angie had brought and sat in the wagon, looking at the pictures and tracing the letters with his fingers. But all the time he was thinking of Jup. The dog couldn't talk so Boss would never know. He had so much more to lose than Jup! Boss would forget about what she thought Jup had done but would she forget that again David had caused trouble? Would she be mad enough to send him away if she knew? Because he didn't know the answers to these questions, he knew he wouldn't tell her and he was ashamed.

For the next few days, he worked hard to make up for the way he felt. He left with Boss and the sheep for the grazing lands in the early morning. Boss assigned him a place in the rear, watching for strays on the long walks. He didn't allow a single sheep to wander away. He covered miles, running back and forth behind the band, as well as moving forward with it. With a switch in his hand, he turned back the sheep that saw a nicer tuft of grass off the path or that stepped aside to investigate a hopping cottontail. He filled the water pails at night, made the fire, washed the dishes, cleaned his boots, and fell into bed exhausted. But what he had done to Jup bothered him and the more he tried not to think about it, the worse it was.

One evening as they brought the sheep in toward the bed ground the dogs broke away and ran to the wagon. Their rough coats stood up stiffly as they raced round and round the wagon, their noses to the ground. By the time David, who was behind the flock, reached the bed ground, Boss was standing on the steps of the wagon.

"Come and see," she called, her face an angry red. He ran to the stairs and looked inside. The wagon was a shambles. The door had been broken in and on the floor were strewn shredded blankets and clothes, a ripped bag of flour, a sack of coffee, and baking powder tins with their lids torn off.

"Look!" Boss cried. "There by the steps is the print where he sat down to look the place over. What nerve!"

"Who?" David asked, wondering who could have done this thing.

"That confounded bear! That devil wrapped in fur! That miserable, ornery, thieving killer, that's who!"

The bear had managed to open the trapdoor on the bench, and his great claws had raked through the supplies, destroying what he hadn't eaten.

After the sheep were bedded down, they

cleaned the wagon as best they could, Boss grunting and snorting when she came upon dark-brown hairs tipped with gray.

"I'll get him some day," she said over and over. "I'll never give up until that bear is dead." The boy had never seen her in such a state. "He's a smart one, all right. He tore up Bezeleel's wagon three times in the past few years. The old man even saw him once at the edge of a clearing."

"Why didn't he shoot him?"

"It isn't allowed. The government protects a grizzly unless he's caught in the act of killing a sheep or raiding a camp. If we'd come back in time to see him doing it, it would have been legal to shoot him. Anyhow I can shoot him on sight now. The government accepts he's a killer. Old Bezeleel didn't have any reason to kill him then, since he didn't catch him causing trouble. But when I find him, I'll finish him off, never fear."

"Would he have come in if I'd been here?" David asked, imagining a thousand-pound bear pushing through the door some day.

"No, he's too smart for that — won't come close to humans if he can help it. You can bet on that. But from now on, I'll be carrying my gun, knowing he's around somewhere."

David was almost glad it had happened. Now maybe Boss would forget about being so mad at Jup.

8

The weather was cold and raw but there weren't any heavy snows in December. When the wind blew, it rattled the bare branches of the trees and swept the shallow powdery snow in swirls through the air. David learned to tie a scarf across his face to protect his nose and mouth and allow him to breathe more easily. On the days the sun shone on the snow, he and Boss wore dark glasses so they wouldn't go snow-blind. They wrapped their potatoes and canned milk in a bed-roll before they left the wagon in the morning, and when they returned at night they often found the water bucket frozen and the stream covered with ice. They were so tired that after bedding down the sheep and a quick dinner, they fell into their beds. Sometimes it seemed to the boy that he had hardly closed his eyes when the dogs let them know it was dawn and the sheep were beginning to stir on the bed ground.

The air was fresh, sharp with the spice of fir trees. The cold and the hard work made David hungry and he began to gain in height and weight so that Ben's clothes really fitted him now. His cheeks filled out and he lost the gaunt look he had brought with him from the crop fields.

The snows that came lay shallow enough on the ground for the sheep to paw their way through to the grass, and the flock began to grow fat and their wool thicker. There was no further sign of the bear and, although Boss carried her gun with her now, she had no occasion to use it.

Sometimes David stayed at the wagon the days Tex was expected. It gave him a chance to study his letters and to reread the pages in the books that he and Angie had gone over together. Best, it gave him a chance to visit with Tex.

Tex had repaired the door of the wagon and replaced the supplies which the bear had eaten or destroyed. On one of these days, when the boy was waiting for him, Tex brought the provisions in, then announced "I've got a surprise."

He went back to his horse and took something from the saddle. Now that they were so far from the road, Tex brought their supplies in bags, which he hung over his saddle, and left the truck at the ranch. Sometimes when he was cutting wood for them, he let David ride the horse, teaching him first how to handle the reins and how to keep his feet in the stirrups while the horse galloped around the meadow.

"It's a gun!" David shouted. "Are we going hunting?"

Tex draped his long body on the steps of the wagon. "Not yet," he drawled, "and not with this .22. I'm goin' to teach you how to use it. With that bear somewhere around, you ought to be able to handle a gun just in case. I've been thinkin' of it for quite a while now."

He took the gun apart first and showed David how to put it back together. Then he showed him how to load it, how to hold it, how to sight down the barrel, and how to pull the trigger.

"We couldn't practice with the sheep around. I figure, too, that maybe Boss wouldn't let you learn, but this once I'm goin' to do what I think is best without askin' her."

The boy knew how skittish sheep were. They were timid and had to be handled quietly. A shot from a gun could send them racing away in panic from the sound and into a pile-up against the first obstacle in their way.

He and Tex went down by the stream, where there weren't any large rocks to deflect the bullets, and Tex showed him how to aim at an old fence post at the edge of a plain beyond the water.

"You've a good eye, Dave," Tex said when they'd finished the first lesson. "A few more tries and you should be a right good shot."

"Can I keep the gun here and practice?"

"No sir," Tex said. "Boss wouldn't like that. But I'll bring it out next week and we'll shoot again."

While Tex was drinking his coffee inside the wagon, David asked him, "How would you shoot a grizzly?"

Tex swallowed the hot coffee. "There's more downright misinformation about grizzlies and how to get 'em than about almost anything else I know. Why, most folks think a grizzly stands up on his two feet and charges a hunter! I've even seen pictures showin' them doin' that. 'Tain't so. A grizzly only stands up on his hind legs when he's curious about somethin', or when he's alarmed. He does it to get a better look, but when he charges he comes at you by runnin' up to you just like Jup would on all four feet. Folks think you can tree a grizzly. Why, he hardly ever climbs trees — the kind you find around here never do, and they don't hibernate, either."

"But how do you shoot them?" the boy asked impatiently.

Tex shrugged. "That all depends. If he's chargin', you try for a shoulder shot. Break his shoulder and you stop his charge. But you've got to be sure to hit him right, because a wounded grizzly can bounce up after he's down quicker than a rubber ball. Then, if you do get his shoulder, you kill him with a heart or a lung shot. If you had a chance, like comin' on a bear who didn't hear you or smell you, you could try for his brain. But creepin' up on him is a pretty risky business. It's his nose and ears that tell him where you are, not his eyes. He can't see too far, usually just what's straight ahead of him."

"Where would you look for him if you were hunting him?"

"Now that's a good question. If there's anything for sure, it's that he won't be where he's supposed to be and he's sure to be where you'd swear he wouldn't be."

"No wonder Boss hasn't found the bear that killed Ben. She's always looking but he isn't even where his tracks are."

"Sure," said Tex. "While you're followin' his tracks somewheres, he's tearin' up your sheep wagon. But if Boss could spend all her time trackin' him, she'd probably find him eventually. 'Course she might just stumble on him one of these days. That's what worries me. I think a grizzly's too big a job for a woman, even a woman like Boss. If Ben, who was a fine shot, couldn't drop him, I doubt that Boss could."

Tex left, promising to bring the gun again soon. Angie didn't have time to come to see them very often now that the wagon was moved farther from the ranch. But it had been arranged that she and Tex were to be there for Christmas. Boss had declared a holiday for Christmas. They'd keep the sheep in the nearby meadow and all have the day together. "If it doesn't storm," Boss said. "We're due a blizzard one of these days. I've never seen such a mild winter as this has been so far."

It turned out Boss hadn't forgotten her anger at Jup. David noticed that she ignored him most of the time, giving her orders to Juno instead. He saw Jup's puzzlement. The dog was proud of his work and he sensed the slight. It hurt David to see him working his heart out, herding the sheep in perfect style, and waiting for a word of praise. When Boss said, "That'll do nicely," to Juno instead, Jup slunk away.

It was only when Boss said the night before Christmas, "I've decided to have Tex take Jup back to the ranch tomorrow. He can scout me another dog to take his place. I'll never trust Jup again," that the boy found the courage to speak up.

"It wasn't his fault when the sheep panicked. I whistled to him the way you do and he thought I was giving him signals." He said it fast and sat on the edge of his bed, clenching his fists and waiting for what would come. It had suddenly become no longer a question of taking care of himself. He had to take care of Jup, too. He couldn't face Christmas feeling so guilty. He'd feel better getting this off his mind.

Boss went on polishing her boots as though she

hadn't heard. Her mouth was set in a straight line and her large hands rubbed the grease into the leather in careful, powerful, circular motions.

He tried again, "Don't send him away, please! He didn't — " She cut him off short.

"Get to bed," she said, without raising her eyes. He did as he was told. When Boss finished her boots, she put on her coat and left the wagon. David wondered if she was making it up with Jup.

The next morning was so busy he didn't have time to worry about what Boss was thinking. He made up the beds, swept out the wagon, carried water from the stream, checked the flags around the bed ground, and was starting for the meadow to check on the sheep when Angie and Tex arrived. They called out, "Merry Christmas" as they came riding over the hill. On their saddles were hampers of food and Angie opened one to show David the pies set on top.

"There's turkey underneath," she said, "and candy and nuts. And maybe I have a package or two." The cold air reddened her cheeks and her brown eyes sparkled as she teased him. "Maybe one even has your name on it."

It was the first real Christmas the boy had ever known. He sat on the bench and watched as Tex put a tiny fir tree on the table and Angie decorated it with small ornaments. Boss unwrapped the cold carved turkey and dressing and heated the gravy on the stove. She set the pies to warm and put some coffee on to boil.

After they had eaten, Angie gave David his presents — a warm sweater she had knitted for him, a pair of long woollen socks, and two books. "You'll be reading them soon," she promised.

Tex gave him a flashlight of his own, with a box of extra batteries. Boss motioned to Tex and he went back to his horse and returned, carrying a rifle. Boss held it in her hands a while before holding it out to the boy. "It's a rifle," she said, "Ben's gun. I figured one of these days I'd teach you how to shoot it." The boy and Tex exchanged glances. "But it's to be kept up there on that shelf and you're never to touch it unless I tell you to. Do you understand? I'll skin you alive if you do."

David didn't know what to think. Was she giving him another chance? Or was she so glad to know she could trust Jup as she always had, it didn't matter about him? He stroked the satin wood of the stock and examined the steel of the barrel. This gun had been well cared for.

Just then Jup barked and the boy leaped to his feet and went to the door. Disappearing diagonally over the hill was Cluny! Jup danced at the door frantically, letting them know he was going after her.

Boss started to get up but David grabbed his

91

coat and cap. "Let me bring her back," he pleaded. This was his chance to show Boss he really wanted to help, that he could do something right. He looked at her, trying to let her know what he was feeling. His look said, "You can trust me now. I want to make up for what I did before."

She nodded.

David caught up his flashlight and was out the door and running toward the hill. Jup was ahead of him and the boy scrambled over the rocks, keeping the dog in sight.

When David reached the top of the hill he saw that Cluny had already gotten herself into trouble. Across a hundred yards of meadow was a rocky wall. Cluny had climbed it, squeezing herself along a narrow ledge and wedging herself on an overhanging rock. She stood there now, blatting plaintively. A tuft of grass grew out of a crack in the rock, and that was what she had seen and gone after. Now, unless she backed up or turned around, she was stuck. David knew that in this one way Cluny was exactly like all other sheep. She wouldn't back up. And as smart as she seemed to be, it probably would never occur to her to turn around and get out the way she'd gotten in. If he or Jup flurried her in any way, she was just as apt to go over the edge, falling and killing herself or breaking her legs.

Jup waited for David's command. The boy sized

up the situation. They couldn't reach her from underneath. Approaching her from the rear might panic her. That left only one choice — to get at her from above. The incline was steep but flat and Jup might manage it. David had seen him rescue strays from impossible places before. If the dog could inch his way down, then drop beside her suddenly and turn her around before she knew what was happening, he could use his eagle look on her to force her along the narrow ledge and down the hill again.

David and Jup climbed the incline above Cluny. David laid his hand on the dog's head. "Down," he said, motioning. "Get her off."

Jup had already figured it out. He flattened his body on the slope and began inching downward. David went back to the ground beneath the rock and watched. For what seemed like hours, Jup crept down, an inch at a time, taking care not to alarm Cluny, spending her time nibbling at the grass and blatting angrily at David.

Clouds came across the sky and it turned darker. There was the feel of a storm coming. The boy waited. Finally, to ease his impatience and nervousness, he walked along the side of the hill away from the rock. Jup was doing nicely and there was nothing he could do to help. He turned on his flashlight and played the light against the side of the hill. Around a bend, he came on the entrance of an abandoned mine. It was a large gaping hole in the side of the hill, the tunnel leading inward, black and mysterious. He went close and shone the light inside. The passageway was long, with timbers lining the sides and supporting the earth above. He hesitated. It would take Jup another half hour anyway, the way he was going, to get to Cluny and turn her around. David had plenty of time to explore the tunnel a short way.

The air inside the mine was heavy and musty. The floor was uneven and David's boots on the stones sent echoes bouncing back and forth. He shivered with excitement. What was ahead? The light skipped through the dark and finally hit a wall. When the boy reached it, he saw that the tunnel went both to the right and to the left. The wall was wet and his hand came away damp and slick. He ought to go back but if he did, he would never know where the tunnel led. Just a little farther, then he would turn around. He chose the way to the left.

After following the light for about five minutes, down the narrow tunnel, he came to what appeared to be an underground room, the tunnel widening out and the wall no longer within his reach. He moved forward, playing the light upward on jutting rocks which formed a ceiling. He hadn't gone more than twenty feet when suddenly there was nothing under his feet and he found himself falling through space. With a crash, his body hit something and he grabbed, wrapping his legs around it. It was a timber, lying crosswise in the shaft, and it creaked beneath his weight. He lay quietly, getting his breath. Then, slowly, he let go with one hand and reached below him to see if he was at the bottom. His hand splashed in water and he withdrew it hurriedly. His flashlight was gone. It had flown out of his hand when he fell, and he guessed it was somewhere in the water beneath him.

Icy blackness surrounded him. There wasn't a sound after the echo of the crash of his fall had died away. The thought of Jup and Cluny flashed through his mind. He should be back there with them, doing the job he had told Boss he would do. Had he failed her again?

He knew it would do no good to shout. He had to get himself out of this fix. Balanced astride the timber, he held tight with one hand. With the other he reached out and found that his fingers brushed the side of the shaft. He shifted hands and reached with the other. It, too, brushed a wall. Now he knew the width of the shaft. The timber lay across it, wedged against the walls. He inched forward and reached out again. The wall was wet and cold. He shivered, realizing he had forgotten his gloves and hadn't missed them until now. What should he do? What could he do? The

95

side of the shaft was smooth. There wouldn't be a chance of getting a foothold and climbing up. When he moved, the timber creaked under him. If it was too old and rotten, the pressure of his body might cause it to crack or break, and he would find himself in the water below. He shuddered at the thought, for he couldn't swim. He crept forward again, stopping and reaching out. Only the smooth damp wall met his fingers.

He doubled up and rested his head on the timber. It was hopeless. Maybe Jup would track him here and find him. He listened hard but there was no sound. The air was old and stale and the quiet wrapped itself around him. He knew he was fooling himself. Jup wouldn't even look for him. Jup was doing a job and nothing would make Jup leave Cluny before he had her off the rock and driven back to the bed ground again. "All right," David said to himself, "you're so smart about taking care of yourself and not expecting anyone else to, let's see you prove you can now."

He thought of the meadow and the sheep and the wagon and Boss, everything that had become his world. He thought that by now Tex and Angie would have left, and Boss would be rounding up the sheep and heading them toward the bed ground. She'd need him to carry the water in and to make the fire.

Thinking about the fire reminded him that

somewhere in his jacket pocket he had matches. He carried them because it was he who always lighted the fire to protect the sheep from the coyotes. He was thankful now that he had forgotten the wool-lined gloves in his hurry to leave the wagon. They'd be hard to take off now, although his hands would have been warmer. His fingers were growing numb so he tightened his legs around the log and rubbed his hands together. The timber creaked dangerously and he hung on, not moving for the next few minutes. Then, carefully, slowly, he loosened one hand and reached into his pocket. The action unbalanced him and for a moment he thought he would fall. He tried again, moving his hand slowly and gripping the timber between his legs as hard as he could. The matches were there. He withdrew them slowly, then felt and found there were three in the box. Clutching the timber with his elbows, he struck one. The flame spurted brightly for a second, then settled down into a dim flicker. Before him the walls of the shaft rose straight and smooth above him, and the water below was black and frightening. He didn't dare look over his shoulder at the other walls. He would have to work his way back and light another match. Putting the box in his mouth, he inched his way backward, the timber groaning each time he moved. Once, as he slid his legs along it, it moved, and for a sickening minute he thought it was ready to slip and fall, carrying him along with it into the dark water below.

It seemed to take hours to move the length of the log. Inch by inch he slid himself backward, stopping between each move to get a new grip with his fingers. When he felt his feet touch the wall, he lighted another match. In the first flare he saw the ladder. It was within his reach, fastened against the wall of the shaft and leading straight up into the darkness. It looked old and rotted but the boy knew it was his only chance. He raised himself on the timber, moving cautiously, one hand against the wall, and swung himself to a sitting position. Then he brought his leg over and sat facing the ladder, the match flickering in his fingers, then going out. He would have to get on the ladder fast. There could be no hesitation. And he would have to do it in the dark. He would need the last match when he reached the top.

His fingers touched the side of the ladder and he leaned forward. Grasping the other side, he held his breath and leaped for it, his feet finding a rung at the water level. The jolt loosened the log and he heard it fall, heard the splash as the water covered it.

On the way up, several rungs were missing. One of them broke beneath his weight and he fell arm's length, hanging there until his feet could find solid wood again. When he reached the top, he pulled himself onto the ground and sat there, shaking.

The last match lighted his way to the tunnel. From there on, he could find his way. He kept his hands on the wet walls and took the first turn to the right. The cool air that he felt immediately came from the opening of the mine, and he began to run. He had to get back before Jup got Cluny to the bed ground!

9

Angie and Tex left an hour after David went for Cluny. There were signs of a storm coming and they had almost ten miles to do on horseback. Far to the north, a dark-blue cloud could be seen and they knew it was rolling over the plains, bringing wind and sleet and snow with it.

"Shall I help you round up the sheep and get them into the pens?" Tex asked.

Boss shook her head. "You get Angie home safely. I can take care of the sheep. I'll have enough time for that before the storm hits."

"What about the boy? Shouldn't he be back by now?"

Boss waved him toward his horse. "He'll be coming over the hill with Jup and that ornery sheep any minute now. You'd best get going."

After they left, Boss, with Juno helping, rounded up the sheep and led them to the sheltered corral and into the pens on the south side of the hill. She shut them in and they lay huddled close together, warming one another, in the icy wind that was beginning to blow the bushes and shake the trees.

It had taken an hour or more to do the job and by the time she finished, sleet mixed with snow had begun to fall. She fought her way against it toward the bed ground just as Jup appeared over the hill, driving Cluny ahead of him. She wondered why the boy lagged behind but she didn't have time to wait for him. Meeting them, she turned Cluny toward the corral and drove her into the protection of the pen.

"David's probably in the wagon now," she thought, as she struggled through the wind to the bed ground. There were flags to take down and roll up and store in the wagon. She could have used the boy's help and it annoyed her that he wasn't on hand. It took her a long time to gather them all, pulling them out of the ground and tying them together so she could carry them.

"It's going to be a real grizzly!" she said aloud as the wind changed direction again, calling the storm by the name given it by those on the plains who knew the strength and fury of such weather. The gnarled cottonwoods and the willows bent toward the ground. Sleet was beginning to coat the branches and powdery snow was covering the sheltered buildings. The wagon shook as gusts hit it from all sides. The high wind seemed to drive into the marrow of her bones.

She called Jup and Juno and took them into the wagon. They would have a good dinner and she would let them sleep in the wagon tonight. With the sheep penned, it would be safe. It wasn't likely coyotes would be out in this weather. They were probably all snugly at home in their dens.

David wasn't in the wagon and she grew alarmed. Where could he be? Why hadn't he stayed with Jup and Cluny? She was worried and angry. "If he's going to keep doing things like this," she thought, "I can't put up with him." She could forgive that day in the meadow when he had confused Jup with his whistling and his hand signals. It was a fool thing any boy who didn't understand sheepherding might have done, although he should have told her about it at once. But he did tell her finally, and she was willing to let it go at that. Disappearing at a time like this and worrying her when she had enough on her mind was something else.

She decided to feed the dogs, then go look for him. With the storm building up there was little likelihood she could find anything, even her own way back to the wagon, she thought grumpily.

When Ben had gone out to do a job, he had done that job. Was it fair, she wondered, always to judge the boy by what Ben would have done? Ben had been born to sheep ranching and by the time he was David's age, he knew all there was to know about it. Still, in a sheepherder's life there was only one way to do a job, the right way. The boy would have to learn that or he couldn't stay.

She let the dogs out and heard Jup begin to bark. Running to the door, she watched as he disappeared into the whirling snow. In a few minutes he returned with David beside him. Salt tears had frozen in little beads about the boy's eyes, and his hands were blue with cold.

"Thank God you haven't had an accident," she said as he came into the wagon. "I was ready to go out looking for you, expecting to find you at the bottom of a ravine somewhere if I found you at all." She saw that he wasn't hurt and her worry turned to impatience with him.

"Where were you?"

The boy was exhausted. He slumped to the bench and sat there, getting his breath.

"Just looking around," he gasped, "looking around some."

Boss stood over him, fighting to check her anger. "And Cluny? You were going to bring her back."

"I — I left her with Jup. He was taking care of her."

Boss exploded. "So that's your idea of being a shepherd, is it? Well, I'll tell you my idea and I want you to listen hard. I thought you might make a good herder, once you got a lot of nonsense out of your head. There isn't room for nonsense when you're taking care of sheep. Sheepherding is one of the hardest jobs in the world. In other kinds of work, a man stays on a job for so many hours and then he's through. In sheepherding, you work every minute of every day and night, and when you sleep you sleep with one ear on the bed ground." Her voice came in gasps, beyond her control.

"You give up everything to keep your sheep alive and in good shape. You know every inch of the range and where there's grass, and you drive your sheep out at sunup in almost any kind of weather, to keep them fat and healthy. You take pride in doing it and your first, last, and only thought is for those sheep. You don't just walk away and start looking around at something else when you're in charge. You walk miles every day to see that they get the best grass there is, and you come back at night, bone weary, to a frozen water bucket and a freezing wagon. You risk your life going after strays, and through blizzards, and fighting off the animals who are always there, waiting for just one careless minute on your part.

"And why do you do it? Because you're in charge of those sheep!" She jabbed him in the chest with her finger. "And their lives depend on you! You live for them! It's a question of loyalty, David, and every good sheep dog has it. And any herder who hasn't got it isn't worth his salt."

She stopped, out of breath. Then she shook her head. "And you haven't got it, boy. You've proved that. I think you picked the wrong name. You'll never make a sheepherder."

David lay in his bed, exhausted and heartsick. The wind howled outside and the windows were white with clinging snow. The words — "you picked the wrong name" — "you'll never make a sheepherder" — pounded in his head. He realized, too late, how completely he had let Boss down. She had wanted to believe in him but he hadn't let her. He knew he wanted to be a sheepherder more than anything in the world. This was the only kind of life he could imagine now. And he liked his name. He was proud of it. But Boss felt he hadn't earned it.

He hadn't said a word when she finished talking. What could he say? He had left Cluny and Jup. He hadn't done his job. There was no use telling her about the mine shaft. It would sound like an excuse — and it was his fault anyway. He shouldn't have been in the mine in the first place. Way back in his mind somewhere he was remembering an overseer at one of the fields, yelling at a worker, "Don't give me excuses, give me action.

If you can't do the job, get out, and I'll find some-one who can." It was too late to give Boss excuses now.

They were awakened just before daylight by Jup scratching on the door, wanting out. He was excited. Without a word, they dressed hurriedly, putting on two pairs of wool stockings under their boots and wrapping wool scarfs around their heads.

They found the gate of the corral had blown open, the lock broken, and several pens were empty. A marker was gone but there was no way of telling how many sheep had gone with it. The rest of the flock waited uncertainly, crowded to-gether, and blatting loudly. David looked for Cluny. She was gone.

Boss tied the gate closed and she and David went to the building where the food was stored. They carried sacks of cottonseed cake and spread the small brownish-green flakes among the sheep in the pens. Then they brought hay and shook it on the floor of the corral and watched the sheep begin to eat.

Boss studied the weather. The wind was still blowing the snow as it fell, and the meadow, the hills, and the mountains were barely visible through it.

"There's nothing we can do today," she shouted, raising her voice above the wind. "Wouldn't have a chance of finding them in this weather."

"But won't they die? Won't they freeze out there?" David almost screamed to make himself heard.

She shook her head. "They can live several days, buried in snow." She indicated they weren't to try to talk any more, and they went back to the wagon. A piece of the roof flapped in the wind. Boss motioned David inside.

"Would you be afraid to climb up and nail that piece down?" she asked. For reply he went to the toolbox at the end of the bench and brought a hammer and some nails back with him. Boss hoisted him up and he crawled along the wagon roof, wind gusts tearing at him like great hands trying to pull him off. He had nailed the piece down when he saw it, or thought he did. It was a large dark shape, moving now just out of his vision.

"I saw the bear! I saw the bear!" he shouted, his voice carrying away in the wind. He edged back to where Boss waited for him, and she lifted him down.

"I saw the bear!" he said, his mouth close to her ear. She stared at him, astonished, and drew him into the wagon. "Don't make sense," she said. "He'd be holed up in this weather. Any animal would. Anyway, Jup and Juno would be going wild if he were around." She looked at the dogs. They

107

lay peacefully on the floor of the wagon, enjoying every minute of this chance at comfort and warmth.

The snowfall was growing heavier again, surrounding the wagon like a thick white blanket through which there was no way of seeing what lay just outside.

Boss stood hesitant, eying the gun on top of the dish cupboard. "Couldn't have been. Might have been a wild horse maybe, or even a deer. Anyway, we couldn't find him now."

The rest of the day she was restless. The word "bear" was enough to ruin a day for her. They were shut in, shut in by a white curtain around the wagon. She went out once to fill the bucket with snow, and the wind knocked her over into a drift.

"It was all I could do to find the steps again and I wasn't more than a foot away from them," she said.

They didn't try to go back to the corral. The sheep had been fed and the snow would satisfy their thirst. They would be restless, being creatures of habit and used to spending the days on the range, but the pens would hold them. All there was to do now was to sit and wait for the storm to pass.

They didn't talk much. Boss had said all she had to say last night, and for her it had been more talk than she usually made in a week. For David there was nothing to say. He looked at his new books, picking out the words he knew and imagining the stories that went with the pictures.

It was a long day and an uncomfortable one.

The dogs were let out and when they returned, they were covered with snow, little beads of ice hanging to their fur. The boy dried them, then sat down beside Jup, his arms about the collie's neck. The dog sat quietly, his eyes on Boss, his body pressed close to David's.

During the night the wind died down and the sheep wagon acted like a ship that had suddenly sailed into calm water. The rocking of the wind stopped, its eerie cry silent, and David awoke immediately to wonder at the strange stillness. He crept out of bed and stood at the door, peering through the cracks in the snow glaze on the glass. It was almost dawn and the scene outside was peaceful. The snowstorm had ended and an ocean of white lay around them, an ocean that had swallowed up all the familiar landmarks, and which lay untroubled and unmarked as far as he could see.

First thing after Boss awoke, they let the dogs out and watched them flounder in the snow. At the foot of the steps Juno was up to her shoulders, and Jup to his chest. They seemed really to enjoy it, leaping into the drifts as they headed for the corral.

Boss cooked breakfast, then they dressed, tying

oat sacks over their boots. Boss took flagpoles out of the bundle, handing one to David. "We'll need them to prod with, to find the sheep buried under the snow." They carried shovels across their shoulders.

It took them quite a while to reach the corral, the boy following in the wake of Boss. They found the sheep blatting loudly, hundreds of different voices raised in objection to this imprisonment. The smell of damp greasy wool was overpowering.

Boss and David carried sheep cake and hay to the pens. Then, after checking to be sure the corral gate was tied securely, they set off with the dogs and their poles to find the lost sheep.

"Stay with me," Boss said, "until we find a few. Then you can take Jup and spread out." Her eyes swept the snow-covered meadow and on beyond, moving from side to side above the woolen scarf that covered her nose and mouth. The air was icy and the dogs' breath turned into steam, hanging about their heads like clouds.

There were places where the snow had piled high in drifts, others where the wind had blown it away, and only a thin powder lay on the ground.

"There's one!" Boss cried, and David followed her to where a small hole in the snow released a thin column of steam. She prodded carefully with the pole to see how far below the surface the sheep lay. Then she took her shovel and dug the loose snow and freed the animal. David expected to see the sheep dead, but it leaped out of its hole immediately, full of life. It kicked up its heels and blatted loudly. Boss examined its coat.

"Sometimes when they get hungry enough, they pluck the wool from their sides, chewing on it because of the grease. We're getting them in time." The hole was lined with ice. The warmth of the ewe's body had thawed the snow and the low temperature had caused the damp walls to freeze.

Juno took over and drove the sheep to where the snow covering was shallow. At once the ewe began to scratch for branches and twigs.

David and Jup worked together. Sometimes there would be six or seven ewes in a hole, the weakest trampled underfoot and usually dead. David worried about Cluny. Would they find her at the bottom of a pile, her life snuffed out by the weight of a dozen younger, stronger sheep?

He shouted to Boss when he finally found her. She was in a hole with several other ewes, but she was still alive. "She's too weak to walk," he called, and Boss came and lifted her gently, carrying her to a resting place near the growing flock in Juno's charge. Jup followed her, nuzzling her face and growling softly.

By noon they had found over thirty. The sheep, pawing and scratching at the snow-covered ground, nibbled at whatever they found. David and Boss took off one of their gloves and pulled sandwiches out of their pockets, eating them while moving on to find more sheep. David shared his with Jup. It didn't occur to him that not long ago he would have stoned a dog who was hungry.

Against a hill they found over fifty ewes lying in a snow cavern. The porous snow allowed them to breathe easily, although they were several feet under. David laughed as they bounded out of their icy prison, their faces sad as ever but their bleats joyous and eager. He stopped laughing when he saw the trampled sheep underneath. The weakest had been smothered by the heavy bodies of the others. Boss's face was grim as she knelt to look at them. Eight were dead in this group alone; one was the black marker.

By the end of the afternoon, they had recovered all the sheep they could find. There were twenty dead in holes in the meadow. Boss skinned them but it meant a sizable loss to the ranch business. Although David was sorry about that, he was sorrier they had to die. Jup and Juno, covered with an armor of ice, drove the sheep to the corral. Boss went with them while David stayed with Cluny and the other ewes who had been too weakened by their ordeal to join the rest.

"I'll be back," she told him. "We'll carry them to shelter then." It was quite a way to the wagon and he wondered how they would manage it.

David looked over the meadow, its smooth, snowy cover of the morning broken now by the many holes where the sheep had been found, where their shovels had dug the animals out. The willow trees were covered with ice and stood like tall icicles, upright at the edge of the pasture. Where the sheep had grazed while waiting for them to finish their work, faded brown-yellow buffalo grass and purple sagebrush lay exposed. Cliffs of rose-colored rocks dusted with white formed a background above the meadow. There wasn't a sign of life before him.

He thought of the vegetable fields, the fruit orchards where he had spent most of his life picking and boxing or sacking the crops. He thought of the shacks and the railroad cars and the pickers' camps where he had lived. He thought of the drainage ditch running through the middle of the camp, and the sea of mud which often took the place of a road. He thought of the ugliness he had known so well and had accepted as the way life had to be.

He looked toward the stream, now covered with ice, and remembered the spigot in the yard of the camp and the thin trickle of precious water to fill so many needs. He remembered Raidy and knew that she would have loved Montana, the sheep, and the dogs. Without knowing it, tears ran down his face and froze instantly. All of a sudden he knew this was what he wanted. This was what he loved. Tex had been right. Why be a loner any more, scratching and clawing his way to food and shelter with no one to care about him? He wanted to belong here. Why hadn't he worked harder to make a place for himself? When they had given the other David the sword and the armor to fight the giant, he had refused to wear them until he had proved himself. But he — the one who had taken that David's name — had worn their clothes, eaten their food, accepted their roof, but had done nothing for them in return. It was time that he tried to help "his people" in some way.

Cluny got to her feet and tottered a few steps. David ran to her and gently turned her back. Boss had said sheep were helpless. They had to be cared for every minute of the time. He understood now.

Boss returned with a broom and a heavy sack, and together they made a stretcher to hold the sheep who couldn't walk. They rolled Cluny into the opened sack and tied the ends of it over the handle of the broom. Together they carried her to the wagon while Jup stood guard over the other three. When they returned, they found two on their feet and Boss told Jup to drive them slowly to the pens. They carried the other one back and into the wagon.

David made beds for the ewes out of old blankets which he laid on the floor, while Boss cooked a thin gruel. After they had been fed they seemed content to rest in the warmth of the room, blatting now and then, their eyes following any movement.

"You take care of them tomorrow while I get the rest out to graze. After two days of being penned up, they'll be wild to get out."

"But the snow," David said, "how will they manage in the snow?"

"They'll manage," Boss answered, "as long as the snow doesn't crust, they can paw their way through to the grass."

10

After Boss left the wagon the next morning, David fed gruel to the two ewes. Then he took the water bucket outside and started to fill it with snow. Glancing toward the corral, he caught his breath. There was a dark form coming from behind one of the buildings. He grabbed the bucket and started up the stairs, looking once more to be sure. It was a horse! He sagged with relief. It was a horse with a saddle on it. Tex's horse. That must have been what he had seen through the curtain of snow from the roof of the wagon. He set the bucket down and ran as fast as he could toward the corral. The horse met him, neighing loudly.

His rough coat was covered with ice, so the boy led him into the corral and removed the saddle. He ran to the building and brought hay and watched as the horse ate hungrily. Then he plowed his way to the wagon, checked on the ewes, and brought a brush and rags back with him.

"Stand still," he ordered and rubbed the animal as dry as possible with the rags. He brushed him until the horse's coat was shining and smooth again.

"Where's Tex?" he asked. The horse nuzzled him. What was Tex's horse doing here?

He heard a shout and turned to see Angie. She was on snowshoes, pushing her way to the corral. A woolen hat was pulled down over her yellow hair, a heavy sheepskin coat around her. Her cheeks were red with cold and tiny flakes of ice hung on her eyebrows.

She panted for breath when she reached him, her eyes growing large when she saw the horse.

"Where is he?" she asked.

"Who?"

"Tex, of course. That's his horse, isn't it? Where is he?"

The boy shook his head. "I just found his horse a while ago. Tex hasn't been here since Christmas."

She leaned against the corral fence wearily.

"Tex started out for here the day after Christmas. He was worried about you when the storm struck. Worried about Boss handling the sheep in all that snow."

David told her about seeing the horse the day

117

after Christmas, and how it had appeared again today. He took her into the wagon and put coffee on to boil. He could tell she was worried and close to tears, though she tried not to show it. The ewes stirred when she came in, raising their heads to look at her. She bent down and laid her face against Cluny's.

"What shall we do?" the boy asked. "Tex must be somewhere out there, lost. How will we find him?"

"He isn't lost, you can be sure of that," Angie said quickly. "Something's happened to him."

"How will we find him?" David repeated. He could hardly stand the look in her eyes. Was she thinking, too, of the bear?

"I don't know," she said, "but we'll try." She gulped the hot coffee, eager to start.

Then David remembered. "I — I can't leave the sheep. Boss left me in charge of them."

Angie's eyes were suddenly cold and angry. "Can't leave two miserable sheep when Tex's very life may be at stake?"

He felt mixed up. After Boss's talk Christmas night, he couldn't just walk out and leave. That had been his trouble before, leaving his job. But Angie didn't understand what being in charge meant — no more than he had understood before.

"Nonsense," Angie cried wildly. "You just get your things on and forget about these sheep.

They'll be just fine here. And anyway, what's two sheep compared to Tex?"

When she put it like that, maybe she was right. "What — what would Ben have done?" he asked. Immediately, he knew it had been the wrong thing to say. Angie's brows came together and she looked at him, annoyed and surprised.

"Why ask me that? You didn't know Ben. What possible difference could it make to you whether Ben would have done this or that?"

It was hard to explain but he tried. "I thought that's what Boss and you wanted me to do. Wanted me to be as much like Ben as I could, do things the way he would have done them. I ask myself that, whenever I don't know what to do, so Boss will like me and let me stay here."

Angie's face softened and she threw her arms around him. "Oh, David, I guess all of us have confused you. We've made you think we wanted something that we don't want at all. No one should try to be exactly like anyone else. Don't you see? We don't want you to try to take Ben's place. We just want you to be you. It's no good trying to be a copy of someone you never knew. We want you to make up your own mind about what is the right thing to do."

When she put it that way, it was easy to make his decision. If he was supposed to be himself, not a copy of Ben, then he had to do what he knew

119

he should do. "Let's take the horse and maybe he'll lead us to Tex. He must have gone back to Tex after that first time I saw him from the roof of the wagon. That's where the horse has probably been — wherever Tex is."

They filled the thermos with hot coffee and Angie put some biscuits into her pocket. They led the horse out of the corral and turned him loose. He set off immediately, lifting his feet high in the snow. It was slow going but Angie and David stayed behind the animal so that he would choose the way. He led them back along in the direction of the ranch for about a mile, then veered off into a stand of trees.

When he stopped at last, as though to say, "I have done my job, now you do yours," there was no sign of Tex. Maybe the horse was lost, too, the boy thought. He looked around. There was nothing here. "Let's lead him out of these trees and maybe he'll take a new start," David suggested. As they were about to move out, a peculiar formation of snow caught the boy's eye. It was at the edge of the clearing and somehow it didn't look like the rest of the snow on the ground. He went over and touched it with his boot and it collapsed in one corner. Falling to his knees, he brushed the snow away and found a blanket underneath. Lifting it, he saw Tex, curled up in an ice-lined hole just as the sheep had been. But on

Tex's right arm were the steel jaws of a bear trap, closed tight. His eyes were shut.

Angie ran to David's side. She stood beside him, looking down at Tex. Her face was white and her hand was over her mouth. "Is he — ?" she couldn't say it. The sound of her voice aroused the man and he opened his eyes. They could see at once that he was in great pain. His lips were drawn tight over his teeth, his eyes hollow. His gaze rested on Angie's face and he smiled weakly. "It ain't really you, is it?" he whispered. "Am I dreamin' again?"

Angie smiled at him tenderly. She didn't even notice that he had used that word again. Opening the thermos, she held it to his mouth, telling David to lift the blanket away. When he did, he saw that the other end of the chain attached to the trap was secured to a heavy log. He knew this was in case a bear stumbled into the trap and managed to get to his feet again and light out, he'd drag the log behind him, leaving a trail for a hunter to follow.

"How do we open it?" Angie asked Tex.

The man shifted his position and winced with pain. "There's a spring. It's got to be released. I couldn't manage it with my left hand. Could have been worse though — could have been that old bear-tamer trap Boss has out here some place. That's got sixteen-inch teeth and a double spring." He shut his eyes again.

121

David studied the spring and knew neither of them had the strength to force it down. "Just a minute," he said to Angie and went off into the woods, returning shortly with a small but stout sapling.

"Let's try forcing it with this," he suggested.

"Of course," Angie cried. "Compress the spring by means of leverage. Oh, bless you, David. I don't seem to have any wits left."

It worked!

Angie cried out, and David took his hand away. It was shaking. Tex groaned, biting his lips until the blood came. Sliding the trap off Tex's arm, Angie turned white, seeing the mangled flesh.

"I — I lost my way in the blizzard," Tex gasped. "I was leading my horse when I fell and my arm hit the pan of the trap. Next thing I knew, it was on my arm. I couldn't pull the log so I tented in the snow. Don't even know how long I've been here. Just managed to scoop out a hole and rig the blanket before I passed out. Thanks for making me take the blanket along, Angie."

Angie took her woolen scarf and tied a knot in the ends. She slipped it over Tex's head and slid it carefully over the injured arm, cradling it. "Don't talk any more," she said. "Save your strength for getting out of here."

David took Tex's good arm, and Angie knelt down, circling his waist with her arm. Together they lifted and finally Tex was on his feet, wobbly and limp, but on his feet. The question now was how to get him out of the hole.

David had been thinking of that. He bent down and started digging. He dug one side of the hole away until it slanted upward in a ramp. Then he ran to the bushes near by and gathered twigs and branches, spreading them on the ramp to give Tex's feet a hold. Grasping the reins of the horse and pulling him forward, he placed them in Tex's left hand.

"Back, fellow," he shouted to the horse, "back up." The horse retreated slowly, throwing his head up and pulling against the stress on the reins. They guided the man up the ramp, supporting him with their arms.

"Good boy," Tex whispered. "That's using your head." He ate part of a biscuit and drank more coffee, the warmth of it bringing some color into his face.

"If David hadn't seen your horse, if he didn't put him in the corral — " Angie shuddered, look-ing at the hole where Tex had lain. "We might never have found you."

They got him on the horse and led him back to the wagon.

When Boss came home with the sheep that eve-ning, she found the wagon crowded. Tex lay in her bed, the two sheep lay on blankets on the floor, and Angie and David sat on the bench. Tex's arm had been bandaged, the sick sheep had been fed, and there was a stew cooking on the stove.

"I'll never forgive myself," Boss said after she heard their story. "Setting that fool trap in the woods. My hunting that bear will be the ruin of all of us yet."

Angie set off early the next morning on snowshoes. The weather was fine, with a morning sun that turned the fields of snow into a glistening, shining world. She would go back to the ranch, returning with the old sleigh that had sat unused in the barn for so long. Tex grumbled about her going. "It isn't my legs that are hurt," he said. "It's my arm, and there's nothing says I can't ride my horse with one arm."

Angie wouldn't hear of it. "Stay right where you are," she ordered. "Looks as if that sun will melt some of the snow today and I'll be able to get fairly near with the sleigh."

David stayed with Tex and the ewes. He had half expected Boss to say something about his leaving the sheep alone yesterday. She didn't. He knew she was blaming herself for setting the trap in the first place. The sheep were better. Cluny struggled to her feet and blatted her complaints.

"Put her in the pen," Tex said. "She'll be fine out there with some sheep cake and hay."

The boy brushed the horse again and fed him.

Then he went back to the wagon and talked to Tex. He told him about losing the flashlight. "I'm sorry," he said. "It was the first one I ever had." Tex wanted to hear more about the mine, and when David finished telling him, he whistled. "That took a lot of nerve!" He grinned, looking like an old man with his several days' growth of beard. "Most folks would panic at a time like that. You didn't. You used your head."

The boy brushed aside the compliment. "I had to get back. I left Cluny with Jup and it was really my job to bring her home again. That's why I had to do it. I didn't have time to be scared."

"Did you get her home?"

David looked miserable. "No. Jup had her here before I got back."

"And I'll bet you didn't tell Boss what happened."

" 'Course not," David said. "I got myself into that jam so I had to get myself out. There wasn't anything to tell when it was over. Nothing except I guess I'm not a very good sheepherder."

Tex reached over with his good arm and ruffled the boy's hair. If he guessed what had happened between David and Boss, he said nothing about it. Instead, he winked. "Guess being a loner develops a lot of grit. When I get that sheep ranch, you can come and work for me." He looked serious. "Dave, I'm goin' after that bear. Boss will never rest easy until someone does, and I don't like to have her tryin' and worryin' about it all the time. It's just as though Ben won't rest easy either until that bear's dead. When my arm gets better, I'm goin' to track him down and find him. I'm goin' to track that killer down and get him."

Angie was back at the wagon by midafternoon. The snow had melted enough for her to come with the sleigh, and she brought a robe and a pillow to cushion Tex's arm.

"She's gonna make a real sissy out of me, yet," Tex said. "Now, what about my horse? Shall we tie him behind?"

"I've thought it all out," Angie said. "We'll leave him here for David and he can come to the ranch for supplies for the next few weeks — or however long it takes you to get well. You won't be able to lift and carry things for a while." She turned to the boy. "We'll expect you on Thursday, David."

The boy was pleased that he would soon be able to see the ranch. "I'll come." Then he remembered that he had never been there. "How will I find my way?"

Tex laughed. "You just get on that horse's back and say 'Home!' That horse is the homin'est animal I ever saw. All you'll have to do is to hang on."

11

They had a few days of nice weather and the snow melted, leaving most of the ground clear, with a few drifts packed against the rocks, and some of the gullies partly filled. The sheep recovered and were taken back to the flock, which now spent the nights on the bed ground again. When David could manage it, he rode Tex's horse around the meadow, and kept him brushed, fed, and sheltered in the corral.

He thought of the bear often and of Tex's decision to go after it when he got well. Boss still carried her rifle with her and spent as much time as ever looking for tracks.

When the day came for him to go to the ranch for provisions, he saddled the horse while Boss and the dogs moved the sheep off to graze.

"You be careful now," Boss called. "And you start back right after lunch. I don't want you losing your way in the dark."

It was an adventure for the boy to go to the ranch. He remembered what Tex had said and called out "Home!" to the horse, then held the reins so loosely that he might as well not have held them at all. The horse pricked up his ears at the word and trotted right off across the meadow, over the hills and pastures until he came to the road through the woods. Out of the woods they cut across a small plain and wound up a hilly road. David remembered this place. It was where he had built the fire when he started off for California. He saw deer in the meadows below and heard a winter bird call from the woods above him.

He heard the sounds of the ranch before he saw it. From far off came the clash of metal from the anvil in the blacksmith's shop. There were dogs barking and the deep mellow tone of a bell, sweet and clear on the morning air. He saw a windbreak of giant cottonwood trees first, screening the house from his view. Then, as he circled them, he glimpsed the white red-roofed house, large and sturdy, surrounded by rocks and clumps of sage-brush. This was where Angie lived. Off to one side was the bunkhouse which was home to the ranch hands, Tex among them. In the yard, he climbed down, surrounded by barking dogs, and walked to the back door of the house and called out. Angie appeared immediately.

"Come in, come in, David." The kitchen had a huge range and its woodbox was filled to overflowing. "Tex has been up since dawn, ringing that bell for you and waiting." David followed her through the dining room where a big oilcloth-covered table ran the full length of the room, and into the living room that was big but sparsely furnished. A round, potbellied stove stood near the wall, throwing off a glow that spread through the room and warmed him as soon as he entered.

Tex was sitting beside it, a book in his lap. His arm was bandaged and there was a grin on his face. He set the book aside. "She's got me studyin', too, Dave.

"Did you have any trouble gettin' here?" he asked. David shook his head. "That horse is better than a homin' pigeon," Tex said. "Hope you took note of your way here. The horse will know how to go but he'll expect you to give directions. Since it's your home he'll be goin' to, he'll feel it's up to you to pick the way."

The doctor had taken care of Tex's arm and had given strict orders that he wasn't to leave the ranch until it healed. Angie, who was getting ready to leave for school, called out, "Tex, aren't you going to put your horse in the barn? David doesn't know where he belongs."

Tex whispered to the boy, "You'd think we were married, wouldn't you? The way she orders me around!" He looked as if he liked it because he grinned as he went outside.

"David," Angie said, coming into the room and

sitting down beside him, "I wanted to talk to you for a minute. Has Tex said anything to you about going after that bear?"

David just looked at her. Tex had taken him into his confidence and he couldn't tell on him.

Angie, however, went right on, noticing nothing. "Well, I think he has some crazy idea of finding that bear when his arm gets well. He's beginning to talk like Boss does about it." She twisted her handkerchief nervously. "I can't stand it. First Ben, and now maybe Tex. And Boss going wild every time she sees a track. It's almost as if that bear is determined to destroy all of us."

David didn't know what to say. Angie stared into space for a minute or two, then got up and patted his shoulder. "If Tex tells you of any plans, let me know. I'll try to talk him out of them." She went into her room, calling back, "Go on outside, David. Tex will show you around the ranch."

He found Tex in the barn. He had led the horse into a stall and was trying to unsaddle him but his injury made him awkward. David leaped forward and did the job.

As Tex took him around the different buildings, he didn't mention the bear and the boy was glad. This way there was nothing to tell. Much as he liked Angie, he had no intention of repeating anything Tex told him. Tex and he had been loners, and even though they were both getting over it now, that didn't mean he was bound to tattle on Tex.

They visited the smokehouse where dense smoke rose slowly from a fire on the dirt floor. Bacon, hams, sausages hung from blackened rafters. Tex showed him the root cellar where vegetables were piled into bins — turnips, carrots, rutabagas, pumpkins, squash. Onions hung from the walls in bunches and a mountain of potatoes was piled on the floor.

They saw the bunkhouse which Tex and the other regular hand used and which the other herders and extra hands would use when they came back in the spring.

They saw the chicken house, the icehouse, the blacksmith shop, and the granary. The ranch dogs followed at their heels during the tour. Tex told David about the lambing camp which was five miles south of the ranch.

"You'll see it in the spring," he said, "when Boss brings her ewes in. That's when they drop their lambs. There'll be plenty goin' on then to get them and all the other flocks ready for the summer range. You'll see the sheep sheared and dipped, and the wool got ready to sell."

"And the bum lambs with two tails and eight legs?"

"Them, too," said Tex.

They collected the supplies Boss needed and

packed them. Then they had lunch and David was ready to leave. Tex hadn't said a word about the bear, not even when they paused in the blacksmith shop to watch the ranch hand at work and to look at the bear traps and guns hung on the wall.

A plan formed in the boy's mind as he rode back to the range. Tex had once said, "There's always people who need you as much as you need them." He knew now that he needed Boss and Tex and Angie. They had become his life and he couldn't imagine leaving them. But did they need him? Maybe they did, to do the job no one wanted anyone else to do. Tex didn't want Boss to go after the bear, and Angie didn't want Tex to. Nobody had told David not to.

He decided to keep a sharp lookout and if he saw the bear or his tracks, he wouldn't tell Boss. He would manage some excuse to get away and track the animal down. And then when he found the bear, what would he do? Well, he'd try for a shoulder shot if it charged. Otherwise, he'd try for a heart or lung shot as Tex had said. He could see it all in his mind. Only one thing worried him — how to get the gun without Boss knowing it.

He dreamed all the way back to the wagon. He'd get Tex to help him skin the bear after he killed it. Then he'd give the skin to Boss. After that she wouldn't have to worry about anything ever again.

For the next week the boy went to the range every day with Boss and the sheep. Slowly they had moved to grazing land farther to the north of the wagon. When they left a grazed pasture behind, the turf was closely clipped. The split lip and the chisellike incisor teeth of the sheep allowed them to eat the grass so close to earth that any other animal would find it impossible to feed in that area until the grass grew again. The trick of keeping good grazing land was knowing when to move the sheep off, before they'd eaten it too close and ruined it forever.

David said nothing but kept a constant lookout for bear tracks. He found none. As Tex had said, "If anything's for sure, it's that a grizzly won't be where you expect him to be." David knew Boss was watching for tracks, too. He could tell she was disappointed when she came back from a trek through the woods one day, her gun in hand. He was sitting quietly, away from the sheep, so as not to disturb their grazing, yet near enough to see if they got into any trouble.

"I'd like to have old Bezeleel's luck for once," Boss said disgustedly, dropping heavily to a stone beside him. "Seems everywhere that man went, he ran into bears."

"Did he shoot them?" David asked.

"Got a beauty one night, in the mountains on the summer range."

"What was it doing? Killing the sheep?"

Boss chuckled. "No. He was standing on his hind feet looking straight into Bezeleel's eyes and breathing in his face."

"Don't make any sense," David said. "Where was Bezeleel? Up a tree?" He knew that a grizzly standing up like that could be nine feet tall.

"Not exactly. He was up in the air, that's where he was. Bezeleel was just a young fellow, and in those days shepherds who took their sheep to the mountains built themselves a kind of platform to sleep on right at the entrance of the corral. They built it about twelve feet high, setting the poles solid in the ground. Called it a tepestra. Mountains are the loneliest place on earth at night — make a man feel small and no account and afraid. Maybe sleeping up in the air made him feel safer. There were lots of grizzlies around in those days. A grizzly can't climb a pole or a tree unless it's big enough for him to get a real hold with his claws, but he gets mighty curious about something he doesn't understand, like a tepestra. So this bear just stood on a rock and rested his chin on the platform and stared at Bezeleel, who was lying there asleep. I wish you could have heard Bezeleel tell it. He said he felt something warm on his face, and when he opened his eyes he was staring right into another pair of eyes. Said it like to have scared him to death."

"What did he do then?"

"He had his gun right beside him — said he never moved so fast in his life. That bear was a beauty, too, at least the skin was. Bezeleel had hit him right between the eyes. That skin was his proudest possession, even after it was old and moth-eaten and he had dragged it around for forty years."

"Would the grizzly have eaten Bezeleel if he could have got to him?"

Boss shook her head. "I don't think the bear was really after him. He was just curious. A grizzly has a lot of respect for man, and most of them leave when they smell one. He doesn't just set out to hunt a man down. It's when he's surprised during a kill or right after it, or when he's wounded, that he's so dangerous. It's then that he'll charge or jump a man in heavy cover. Why, do you know that a grizzly will hang around a kill he's made but can't eat at one sitting until he's had time to finish it? He'll even bury it and stand guard, and if anyone comes on him then, they'd better watch out."

David was glad to hear her talk. If he was going to get that bear, the more he knew the better. "Do they all kill sheep?" he asked.

"Some do, but this one that's been hanging around this area never has as far as I know. Of course, I guess no grizzly would turn down a piece of meat that walked right up to him, especially in winter when food is hard to find, but he's never raided the flock."

David went to the ranch again the next Thursday. Tex was feeling fine and was impatient to get back to work. "Won't be long now," he said. "I'll be ridin' out soon with the provisions. I'll use Angie's horse and bring mine back then." He didn't say anything about the bear but there was that far-off look in his eyes. David knew if he was ever going to get the bear, it would have to be soon.

A blizzard came down on them on Saturday. He and Boss stood on a hill and saw the dark-blue cloud far away, rolling across the plain. "Let's get the sheep in!" Boss shouted.

Snow was beginning to fall in a heavy swirling mass and the temperature had dropped about thirty degrees by the time they reached the corral. It had been a race all the way, with both of them and Jup and Juno "dogging the sheep" to get them home. On the way Cluny had taken it into her head to leave the flock and had run into a wire fence. The wire cut through her wool and into the flesh, leaving a red stain on her neck.

Boss took off her scarf and wrapped it around the ewe's throat. "She's always the one who gets into trouble," Boss said, pulling her coat up around her neck. David knew that only for Cluny would she give up her scarf, that without it the cold wind was harder to endure.

They tied the gate of the corral securely and fought their way to the wagon. Jup and Juno were ahead of them, wagging their tails happily. They knew in this kind of weather they would be allowed to sleep in the wagon.

During the night, David heard Boss coughing. By morning, she could speak only in a hoarse, rasping whisper. She was stubborn though and insisted on going with David to feed the sheep. They clung to each other in the wind and before they had gone five feet, the wagon was lost behind the swirling snow.

"Won't do," Boss said hoarsely. "Turn back." They groped ahead of them for the steps and finally found them. "Hold on," she said, then crawled underneath the wagon and disappeared. When she came out, she had a coil of rope in her hand. She tied one end of it securely to the wheel of the wagon, then started off with the rest, motioning David to follow her. She played the rope out as they struggled toward the corral. It took them quite a while to find it. David kept his hand on the rope as they went along. When they reached the pens, Boss tied the rope to the fence. They fed the sheep and the boy took care of the horse. Then they fought their way back to the wagon, holding onto the rope, their breath whipped from their mouths and tears freezing in little beads about their eyes.

Boss clutched at her chest when they were inside again, her face crimson, her voice gone.

"You're sick," David said. "Go to bed. I can do anything else that has to be done today." She didn't argue with him as he had expected, and this alarmed him. What could he do for her? He hunted through the cupboards but found only medicine for the sheep, and the antiseptic which had been used on Jup's wounds and on Tex's arm.

By the time he turned around, Boss was fast asleep, her breathing heavy and her face flushed with fever.

12

The storm lasted three days and Boss awoke only to drink the soup and tea the boy fixed. He made his way to the pens every day, holding onto the rope. He fed the sheep and cared for the horse, but the hours were endless and he spent most of them with his books and thinking about the bear. Jup and Juno went with him to the corral, then came back, covered with snow and ice, to lie on the floor of the wagon, their eyes fixed mournfully on the bunk where Boss lay.

The morning of the fourth day was clear and quiet. The snow had stopped early the evening before and the winds during the night had blown it into drifts, leaving patches of ground showing here and there. David knew he must get the sheep out and graze them close to the wagon. As long as they didn't flounder into drifts or stray they would be all right.

Jup and Juno herded them from the corral and

he watched the band spread out as the ewes pawed through the snow, and moved on to find what leaves or twigs still lay on the ground. To give them enough to eat and keep them content, he brought cottonseed cake and scattered it on the ground in a row across the meadow. Then he spread pea straw on the snow. It was noon by the time he finished and he returned to the wagon to see how Boss was.

She was lying on her bed, awake, waiting for him. He told her what he had done. She smiled weakly.

"I don't know what I'd have done without you, David," she said. The boy flushed with pleasure. It was the first compliment she had ever paid him. She didn't add, "I was wrong about your not being a sheepherder." She didn't need to say it. Boss said so little that whatever she said was worth ten times what anyone else might say.

After he fixed lunch, he went back to the sheep. A small number were grazing too near the willows and he decided to turn them back toward the rest of the flock. He found Jup there, running back and forth, his nose to the ground. Juno struggled through the snow at the far edge of the pasture, watching for strays.

He followed Jup and found the dog was tracking a sheep, the prints leading into the woods. At once he knew it must be Cluny. Only she would be

140

brave enough to explore that strange place alone. He motioned Jup to take the other ewes back to the band and went into the woods for a short distance, following the ewe's trail. Then he saw it. A fresh bear track! His heart beat fiercely and he wasn't sure whether it was from excitement or fear. Following Cluny's trail, he went farther into the willows and found more bear tracks.

It had happened! Just when he had almost given up, the bear had appeared again. This might be the only chance he would ever have to find the grizzly. Tex would be starting his hunting as soon as the snow cleared enough for him to get through from the ranch.

If only he were in time to save Cluny! Apparently the bear was desperate for food in this weather and had come to raid the flock. He must decide what to do. He was in charge of the sheep. Did he have the right to leave them? For all he knew, the bear might be circling around right now to attack them from the other side of the hill. Should he send Jup after Cluny? It seemed to him he was always having to make up his mind about leaving the sheep. Should he let Ben settle it for the last time? It seemed a good idea so he asked himself again, what would Ben do? The answer seemed to come clear and sharp, as though someone had spoken it. "Get the bear!"

Jup was worried about Cluny. He came back to

the edge of the woods and looked at David. "Get back!" the boy said. "I'll fetch her myself."

He went to the wagon and opened the door cautiously. This was no time to alarm Boss. She was too sick to be bothered about a bear now. He would tell her Cluny had strayed, if she asked, and that he was going after her. Somehow, somehow, he would have to get the gun.

She was asleep, her face turned toward the wall of the wagon. Quietly he climbed up and got the rifle and the box of ammunition. He was holding the gun by the small of the stock and about to go out the door when he heard her turn over. He looked back quickly and saw that her eyes were open. Without a word, he fled, out the door and across the pasture as fast as he could.

Waving Jup away, he started into the woods, studying the trail Cluny had left — on the lookout also for bear tracks. As he went deeper among the trees, the snow disappeared from the ground and it was hard to find a trail to follow. He crept through the willows, his ears straining for sounds, his eyes busy. On a sharp low branch he found a tuft of wool. Farther on, the outer branches of some underbrush were grazed bare. Cluny had come this way. Of that he was certain.

It was strange there in the woods. The trees seemed to press in against him and he felt stifled. He began to shiver and he stopped to get hold of himself. The gun was heavy and the box of ammunition got in his way, so he sat down and loaded the rifle, setting the box at the foot of a tree.

He knew he couldn't wait if he were to save Cluny. Also, if Boss had seen the gun in his hand, she would follow him. She would guess what he was doing and, sick or not, she would follow.

He heard a sound and held his breath. It came from somewhere ahead of him. Standing up, he moved slowly forward, the gun ready in his hand. He saw a small clearing ahead and crept toward it. Flattening himself behind a tree, he peered out. Something gray-white and woolly caught his eyes, something that had been Cluny. There was blood on her coat and the sight sickened him. At last Cluny had paid for her strange ways. Cluny had had the heart of a lion. She had ventured where none of her sister ewes would follow. She had been ornery and curious and brave, and David knew he had loved her. All the anger he had felt in his life rose up in him. It was the anger of the weak against the strong, the same anger he had felt when the man in the filling station had called him "trash" and had threatened him.

It built up into an overpowering fury inside of him, and he stepped from behind the tree, ready to face anything. He saw the bear. It was returning to its kill. The bear saw him at the same time. Rising on its hind feet, it stared at him, its small nearsighted, red-rimmed eyes curious, its head weaving from side to side. It was the biggest animal David had ever seen. The brown fur, tipped with gray, was shaggy and thick. Its body was a mountain of flesh with a large hump between the shoulders. He remembered what Tex had said — when the bear was ready to charge he would drop to all four feet. He cocked the rifle and put his finger on the trigger. He would aim for the shoulder and hope.

Something passed him in a flash, to lunge at the bear. It was Jup, his black-and-white coat bristling, his teeth bared wickedly. Jup hadn't been able to stand it. He had left Juno in charge of the sheep and had come after Cluny.

Jup flung himself upward, his sharp teeth digging into the skin between the bear's eyes. The bear's great jaws were open wide and he bellowed in surprise and rage. David felt his hair rise. It was the loudest, most horrible noise he had ever heard. The grizzly stepped backward, Jup's body lashing through the air as he kept his hold. Maddened, the bear raised his paw and raked the side of the dog with his claws, but Jup held on. The boy didn't dare to shoot.

Furiously the bear weaved from side to side, shaking his great head, trying to get rid of the dog. A voice, somewhere behind the boy, cried, "Jup, let go!" The dog let go, falling to the ground and leaping into the brush, safe from the swipe of the bear's tremendous paws.

This was the chance David had been waiting for. He knew now that Boss had caught up with him, that she stood behind him, ready to snatch the gun from his hands. There wasn't a moment to lose. He must act before the bear dropped to all fours and made his charge. Free of the dog, the grizzly still stood erect, furious at the attack that had been made on him, furious to have been disturbed after his kill. His great mouth was wide open and he was bellowing hideously.

David leaped forward, stopping right in front of the bear. He raised the rifle and sighted as Tex had taught him. His aim was upward, into the bear's mouth, into the brain. Praying the gun would remain steady, he squeezed the trigger. The shock sent him backward into Boss's arms. The gun fell to the ground. Ahead of him, the bear reeled at the impact of the bullet, stood still for a moment, then slowly crumpled to the ground. The shoulders sagged, the breath came loudly in a sighing noise, the hind legs relaxed and stretched out behind. Then there was no sound, nothing. There was only the beat of David's racing heart and the feel of Boss's arms around him.

He turned and pressed his face into her body. She held him close, steadying him, patting him on the back.

"You hit his brain, David!" she cried. "One shot and you hit him right in a vital spot!"

He cried out wildly, "I had to do it. I had to kill him — for you — and Tex and Angie. I had to do it myself."

Her laugh was a nervous, choking sound. She rocked him in her arms and he felt she was crying. Boss, big and strong as a man, was crying — crying just like a woman.

He clung to her for a few minutes, then pulled away. "Where's Jup? We'd better see how he is."

They found him lying in the brush among the trees, his side raw with ripped flesh, his fur torn to ribbons.

David went back for a shovel and they buried Cluny. Together they carried Jup home. Once back in the wagon, Boss fell on her bed, her face white, her whole body shaking.

"You shouldn't have come," David said. "You shouldn't have followed me. I knew I could get him. I knew I could."

Boss smiled weakly. "I knew you could, too, David. But you can't blame me for wanting to see you do it, can you?"

The winter was over. David sat on a rock and watched the sheep. The warm wind of spring, the chinook, swept down from the Rocky Mountains and across the valley and plains. The hills were

146

turning a pale green, the sweet fragrance of fir and spruce and pine was on the air, and everywhere there was life beginning again. Above him an eagle soared through a cloudless sky, and somewhere off in the distance he heard the song of a meadowlark.

The sheep grazed happily on buffalo grass, sage, cheat grass, bluegrass. Their coats were thick and shaggy, their bodies heavy. Next week he and Boss would get things in order, clean the pens, check the food still on hand in the buildings, then together they would drive the ewes back to the ranch for lambing. He thought of Cluny and how there would never be another ewe like her. He missed her.

Jup stood at the outskirts of the flock. He had paid dearly for his part in killing the bear. It had taken him a long time to recover from his wounds. And Boss had been back on her feet for a month before he was. Now he had only the use of three legs, one of his hind legs would always be crippled. The tendons had been severed by the bear's claws. Still he was doing his job, more slowly perhaps, but still on the alert, guarding his flock of sheep as usual.

The day after the bear was killed, Tex had managed to get through the snows and to the wagon. After one look at Boss and Jup, he had left, returning with Angie and medicines.

They hadn't believed David at first when he told them about shooting the grizzly. "Tell me again," Tex had insisted, and he had listened, shaking his head in amazement. "That's the craziest way of killing a grizzly I ever heard of," he said, slapping his legs. "Standing in front of him and blowing his brains out. What would you have done if you'd missed?"

"He didn't miss," Boss said, raising herself on her elbow. "I've been lying here thinking about it — and you know what it reminds me of? David in the Bible, facing up to that giant Goliath with only a stone in his slingshot. Our David was just like him — he knew he wouldn't miss."

David looked at Angie. She was smiling at him.

Tex and David had gone back to where the bear lay. "It's a fine skin," Tex said admiringly as he looked it over. "Now, unless we want the coyotes to ruin it, we'd better get to work on it."

They skinned it, brought the hide back to the corral and green-salted it. The cold air would keep it until Tex could take it back on his horse. "That hide will square about seven feet," Tex said.

"What does that mean?" David asked.

"Ready for a lesson in arithmetic? Well, you measure the length from the tip of the nose to the tip of the tail. Then you measure between the front paws. Add those two figures together and divide what you get by two. I'd say this fellow is about eight feet long and six feet wide so he'd square at seven feet. And that's a hide to be proud of, David. A real whoppin' fine hide!"

David watched Jup now in the meadow. Boss said, "Nothing can kill that dog. But next year he'll stay at the ranch with us, David. He's earned a rest."

The boy wondered if Jup knew why Boss had taken Juno to the ranch today. Did he know he was going to be a father? Boss had said David could pick out any pup he wanted. It would be his own dog to train, to work the sheep with him.

Boss would also arrange with Tex to bring horses to pull the wagon back to the ranch. It was time to leave the winter range. He looked about him. It all seemed so peaceful and quiet now. To look at it, no one would believe the dangers that were always there. A blizzard in winter could be as deadly as an angry grizzly. Hungry coyotes could snatch the ewes out of the flock. Deadly weeds pushed up through the earth in spring-time — the death camas, the lupine, the larkspur which poisoned and killed the sheep. And the lo-coweed which drove them crazy.

City folks, people who didn't know any better, would look at the flowers and think how pretty they were. It took a real shepherd to know what they could do to a flock.

Even the birds were a threat. The magpies stole

rides on the ewes' backs, pecking at open wounds or pecking the eyes out of new lambs. The eagles could easily carry off a lamb or attack a full-grown sheep, killing it by striking it over and over again on the neck.

Sheep had to be taken care of. A fat ewe could fall and roll onto her back, and because she couldn't get up by herself, she could starve to death or a buzzard could finish her off. Sheep were timid by nature and a loud unexpected noise could send a whole flock into a pile-up. There was no end to the things that happened to sheep unless they had a shepherd who cared more about them than about anything else in the world.

David was proud. Proud that Boss left him now in complete charge of the flock. He knew he and Jup could do as good a job as any herder.

He climbed down and whistled to the dog. Raising his arm, he signaled for the sheep to be rounded up and headed back four miles to the bed ground. The sun was low in the sky and Boss would be in the wagon, waiting for him. He would be able to see the smoke from the chimney long before he reached it. There would be dinner waiting and maybe a pie Angie had sent back with Boss.

As he walked, he thought of Raidy. She had been the first person he had known who bothered to love and care for those who needed her. It had been Tex who had taught him how to stop being

150

a loner, how to throw in his lot with others and work for everyone, not just for himself. It had been Angie who had believed in him and helped him to believe in himself. And it had been Boss who had shown him what loyalty meant — loyalty to the sheep, to the job he had to do.

"Co-o-o-oh," he called to the stragglers, shifting his canteen to his other shoulder.

As he walked behind the sheep, he thought of all that lay ahead. Tex and Angie would be married this summer and live at the ranch with him and Boss until Tex could get that ranch of his own. Next winter there would be a new herder to take over the wagon on this winter range while David went to school and helped Tex with the ranch chores. He would have his own puppy and there would be the new lambs. Perhaps among them there might be another Cluny. He would learn about the shearing, the dipping, how to drive the sheep to summer range high in the mountains.

The bearskin on the wall of the ranch house meant Ben could rest easy now, that all of them could rest easy.

Yes, next week he would be going home, home to the ranch. Home was a special word to a loner, to a bum lamb. It rang clear and sweet like the bell Tex had rung to guide him to the ranch. It said, "This is where you belong."

"Turn them to the bed ground," he shouted to Jup. "Bed them down!"

🍎 **APPLE**®PACKERBACKS

ADVENTURE!
MYSTERY!
ACTION!

Exciting stories for you!

☐ MN42417-3	**The Adventures of the Red Tape Gang** Joan Lowery Nixon	**$2.75**
☐ MN41836-X	**Custer and Crazy Horse: A Story of Two Warriors** Jim Razzi	**$2.75**
☐ MN44576-6	**Encyclopedia Brown Takes the Cake!**	**$2.95**
	Donald J. Sobol and Glenn Andrews	
☐ MN42513-7	**Fast-Talking Dolphin** Carson Davidson	**$2.75**
☐ MN42463-7	**Follow My Leader** James B. Garfield	**$2.75**
☐ MN43534-5	**I Hate Your Guts, Ben Brooster** Eth Clifford	**$2.75**
☐ MN44113-2	**Kavik, the Wolf Dog** Walt Morey	**$2.95**
☐ MN32197-8	**The Lemonade Trick** Scott Corbett	**$2.95**
☐ MN44352-6	**The Loner** Ester Weir	**$2.75**
☐ MN41001-6	**Oh, Brother** Johnniece Marshall Wilson	**$2.95**
☐ MN43755-0	**Our Man Weston** Gordon Korman	**$2.95**
☐ MN41809-2	**Robin on His Own** Johnniece Marshall Wilson	**$2.95**
☐ MN40567-5	**Spies on the Devil's Belt** Betsy Haynes	**$2.75**
☐ MN43303-2	**T.J. and the Pirate Who Wouldn't Go Home** Carol Gorman	**$2.75**
☐ MN42378-9	**Thank You, Jackie Robinson** Barbara Cohen	**$2.95**
☐ MN44206-6	**The War with Mr. Wizzle** Gordon Korman	**$2.75**
☐ MN44174-4	**The Zucchini Warriors** Gordon Korman	**$2.95**

Available wherever you buy books, or use this order form.

Scholastic Inc., P.O. Box 7502, 2931 East McCarty Street, Jefferson City, MO 65102

Please send me the books I have checked above. I am enclosing $_____ (please add $2.00 to cover shipping and handling). Send check or money order — no cash or C.O.D.s please.

Name _____

Address_____

City _____ State/Zip _____

Please allow four to six weeks for delivery. Offer good in the U.S. only. Sorry, mail orders are not available to residents of Canada. Prices subject to change.

AB991

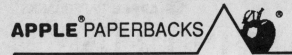

APPLE® PAPERBACKS

Pick an Apple and Polish Off Some Great Reading!

BEST-SELLING APPLE TITLES

❑ MT43944-8 **Afternoon of the Elves** Janet Taylor Lisle $2.75

❑ MT43109-9 **Boys Are Yucko** Anna Grossnickle Hines $2.95

❑ MT43473-X **The Broccoli Tapes** Jan Slepian $2.95

❑ MT40961-1 **Chocolate Covered Ants** Stephen Manes $2.95

❑ MT45436-6 **Cousins** Virginia Hamilton $2.95

❑ MT44036-5 **George Washington's Socks** Elvira Woodruff $2.95

❑ MT45244-4 **Ghost Cadet** Elaine Marie Alphin $2.95

❑ MT44351-8 **Help! I'm a Prisoner in the Library** Eth Clifford $2.95

❑ MT43618-X **Me and Katie (The Pest)** Ann M. Martin $2.95

❑ MT43030-0 **Shoebag** Mary James $2.95

❑ MT46075-7 **Sixth Grade Secrets** Louis Sachar $2.95

❑ MT42882-9 **Sixth Grade Sleepover** Eve Bunting $2.95

❑ MT41732-0 **Too Many Murphys** Colleen O'Shaughnessy McKenna $2.95

Available wherever you buy books, or use this order form.

Scholastic Inc., P.O. Box 7502, 2931 East McCarty Street, Jefferson City, MO 65102

Please send me the books I have checked above. I am enclosing $_____ (please add $2.00 to cover shipping and handling). Send check or money order — no cash or C.O.D.s please.

Name_____ Birthdate_____

Address _____

City_____ State/Zip _____

Please allow four to six weeks for delivery. Offer good in the U.S.A. only. Sorry, mail orders are not available to residents of Canada. Prices subject to change.

APP693